Intaglio

A Novel in Six Stories

Roberta Fernández

WITHDRAWN

Arte Publico Press
Houston
Texas
1990

D0109026

Permission to quote from the following is greatfully acknowledged. Excerpt from *The Ethnic Origins of Nations*, by Anthony Smith. Oxford: B. Blackwell, 1987.

Excerpt from "Holiday Traditions Meld Generations" by Ellen Goodman. Used by permission from the author.

Excerpt from *In Search of Our Mothers' Gardens*. Copyrighted 1974 by Alice Walker. Reprinted by permission from Harcourt Brace Jovanovich, Publishers.

Excerpt from *Dangerous Music*. Copyrighted 1976 by Jessica Hagedorn. Reprinted by permission from Momo's Press.

Excerpt from *Obras Completas* by Pablo Neruda. Buenos Aires: Editorial Losada, 1968.

Excerpt from "Three Songs to Mark the Night" by Judith Mountain Leaf Volborth. In *That's What She Said: Contemporary Poetry and Fiction by Native American Women*. Bloomington: Indiana University Press, 1984.

Excerpt from "With No Immediate Cause" by Ntozake Shange. Used by permission of the author.

Excerpt from "Romance Sonámbulo," *Romancero Gitano* by Federico García Lorca. Mexico: Editorial Diana, 1964.

Excerpt from *Emplumada* by Lorna Dee Cervantes. Reprinted by permission from the University of Pittsburg Press, 1981.

A special thanks to the MacDowell Colony in New Hampshire for its own kind of nurturing during two residencies, in 1983 and 1988; and to Ellen MacCracken, for an editor's reading of the entire manuscript.

Cover art: "Quinceañera" by Rosario Azíos.

Fernández, Roberta.
   Intaglio: a novel in six short stories / Roberta Fernández.
   p.   cm.
   ISBN 1-55885-016-3
   1.Title.
   PS3556.E72425I58 1990
   813'.54–dc20   90-360
                                                         CIP

The paper used in this publication meets the minimum requirements of the American National Standard for Permanence of Paper for Printed Library Materials Z39.48-1984. ∞

Copyright ©1990 Roberta Fernández
Printed in the United States of America

intaglio (ĭn-tăl'-yō)

1. an engraving or incised figure in stone;

2. a figure depressed below the surface of the material and having the normal elevations of the design hollowed out so that an impression from the design yields an image in relief;

3. the art or process of executing intaglios; the process of being imprinted upon.

In Memoriam

For my mother, Margarita López Fernández, who simmered the myths of two cultures in a simple earthen pot, then nourished me with spoonfuls of her seasoned sauce.

... in a 'traditional' society, one was expected to fashion one's life-style and ambitions in terms of collective traditions, so that there was little need to yearn for a past that was being continued. ... nostalgia for one's ethnic past has become more acute and more widespread and persistent in the modern era. ... All that is left is memory and hope, history and destiny. But these memories and hopes are collective and inter-generational; they are *'our'* history and *'our'* destiny.

> Anthony Smith, *The Ethnic Origins of Nations*

... tradition is not just handed down but taken up. It's a conscious decision, a legacy that can be accepted or refused. Only once it's refused, it disappears.

> Ellen Goodman, "Holiday Traditions Meld Generations"

They dreamed dreams that no one knew—not even themselves in any coherent fashion—and saw visions no one could understand. ... Our mothers and grandmothers, some of them moving to music not yet written.

> Alice Walker, *In Search of Our Mothers' Gardens*

TABLE OF CONTENTS

Andrea

something about you
all of us
with songs inside
knifing the air of sorrow
with our dance
a carnival of spirits
shredded blossoms
on the water

Jessica Hagedorn

Andrea's Family

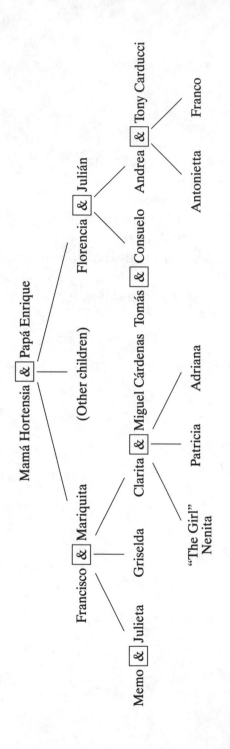

Andrea

I

The most extraordinary images of Andrea had been
neatly mounted inside the black triangular corners in the
thick blue album. It had taken my mother almost fifteen
years to piece all those pictures together; after that, she
had carefully guarded her collection for almost as long as
it had taken her to assemble it. She was so attached to her
album that for as far back as I could remember she had been
telling my sisters and me all about her cousin Andrea's dramatic life. My mother's retelling had made us very aware
that the backdrop for Andrea's adventures had been set a
long time ago, even before she had made her debut at the
Teatro Zaragoza.

The photographs were our connection to that past. At
first my mother had stored them in a large hat box but soon,
the constant arrival of Andrea's parcels caused it to over-
flow. The postmarks on those packages indicated that she
had been in San Francisco and Santa Fe, Tucson and Albu-
querque, cities my mother knew only from magazines and
the movies. Mother was so good at describing those places,
however, that I soon began to imagine myself journeying in
Andrea's footsteps.

The album on Andrea's career had actually initiated me
in this ritual already, for it had helped me and my sisters
relive Andrea's experiences over and over. Andrea had assisted with this rerun by jotting on the back of each program

or photo the information she thought my mother wanted to know: the name of the production, where it had been performed and the role she had played in it. Between the two of them, they had constructed a significant record of our family's history.

Over the years, the performer in the picture book had acquired a special quality for all of us; yet, in fact, my sisters and I knew Andrea only as the flamboyant character in the photographs. The last time she had visited my mother and my aunts, Patricia had been an infant and Adriana hadn't yet been born. I had been so little then that the only thing I remembered about her was a softly melodious voice which slowly became transformed into an enchanting personality who traipsed about in the limelight of make-believe and far-away.

But now she would be coming to see us once again. Tía Griselda and Tía Julieta had just told us that Andrea's visit would coincide with Violeta Aguilera's dance recital and knowing that Andrea would be in the audience during my first solo performance had really unsettled me. So, I barely listened to Tía Griselda's comments as she started to turn the pages of the album. By the tone of her voice in the background, though, I knew she had assumed the role of mother's elder sister as she described her early life in San Luis Potosí. As she talked, I preferred to concentrate on the sounds in my head—the steady clatter of castanets and Violeta Aguilera's strict counting of the *paso doble*.

Still, I was unable to completely drown out the sound of Griselda's voice as she pointed to a portrait of Andrea's family. "Here's the entire family at Andrea's baptism. The picture captures the family relationships very well. There's Florencia holding the infant Andrea in her white baptismal gown. Notice how her gaze is letting the whole world know that this child was to be the center of her world. And here is Julián, the girls's father. See how he has his arm around

Consuelo. They were very close to each other. For ten years Consuelo had grown up as an only child. Her father's favorite daughter you might say. The picture was taken in 1910. A few months later, they all headed northward. So while Andrea spent all her childhood in this country, Consuelo arrived fully formed. She was a very serious child and people tended to attribute her solemnity to an inability to adjust to a new culture. But you can tell from this picture that already in Mexico she had a very serious bent."

As soon as Griselda mentioned the expression on little Consuelo's face, the music in my head came to a stop. For some reason, every time I looked at this particular picture I became intrigued with the look on Consuelo's face. The sharp contrast it made with the dimpled, smiling seven-year old Andrea in the picture on the facing page could not be greater.

In the second picture, Andrea was standing in front of one of the large-framed houses at the local army compound. The house belonged to Mrs. Anderson, who taught piano classes in the local schools while her husband did his military duty. The third person in the photo was Mrs. Bristol, a poet of sorts from Connecticut. I knew that when Consuelo was thirteen she had done some housework for Mrs. Bristol and that the two women had taken it upon themselves to support Andrea's obvious talents by sending her to classes taught by the well-known dancer Pepita Montemayor.

I did not need to listen to Griselda's narrative to know she was not particularly fond of either Mrs. Anderson or Mrs. Bristol; so, I tuned her out altogether as the music once again filled my head. Instead, I pictured us—Pepita, Andrea, Violeta and me, four generations of dancers—moving to the sounds of the *jota aragonesa* as the steady, rhythmic chatter of eight castanets exploded in a crescendo over and over again.

The colorful ritual in my head ended when my sisters

burst into laughter as they pointed to a picture of Andrea and Tía Julieta as young girls wearing long tunics tied at the waist with a cord.

"So you think we look funny?" Julieta asked them. "Well, let me tell you, we were marvelous in this *pastorela*. 'La Aurora del Nuevo Día'. We performed it at the St. Agustine Church plaza in 1921 when we were both eleven. Andrea convinced me to be her partner. I'm glad she did, since it's been my only performance in theater."

Griselda pointed to two more pictures. "Here, she's already at the Royal Opera House. In this picture, she's an Aragonese and in there, she's a *Tehuana*, a woman from Tehuantepec. She was thirteen then. Look at her *tehuana* headpiece. It's all made of lace and shaped like a huge balloon. Only her face showed through the opening. To me she looked like a smiling sunflower."

"Can we look at the picture of Doña Inés?" little Adriana piped in. "It's my favorite."

"You mean this one?" Mother turned to the back of the album, pointing to a photo of Andrea in a floor-length outfit and long curls gathered into a big cluster.

"That's my favorite," Adriana nodded.

"This one was taken at a theater in New York. Andrea appeared there in 'Don Juan Tenorio.' It was her last performance. November the 2nd, 1940."

"I'll show you the one I like the most," I said flipping through the pages. "I just love the way she's looking at us here. See how her hands are crossed at the back of her neck. Look at her funny little heart-shaped mouth. How I'd love to be wearing that long sequinned dress!"

"Hmmm," began Griselda. "She looks too artificial. The real Andrea was never like that. Today, she probably has no connection to that look. It's been fifteen years since she left the theater and that's really a long time to be away from all this."

"You're right. She is another person now," mother agreed. "The contrast was very obvious in the snapshot she sent us last Christmas."

"I remember. They looked like they were having lots of fun in the snow," Patricia interjected. She looked at mother with admiration, then asked, "How did you ever put so much work into this album? Me, I get bored with scrapbooks right away. But, Mama, you just kept making this one bigger and bigger. Didn't you ever get tired of it?" A wistful expression settled on mother's face. "You can't begin to imagine how much I loved touching all the material that kept coming in. Year after year. Sometimes when I was down in the dumps, the mailman would surprise me with a thick package. I never knew when it would arrive. But whenever it got here I'd show the materials to Mamá and Griselda and Julieta." She paused for a moment. "There was always such a sparkle in Andrea's face. For hours and hours we'd look at the pictures, imagining what her life must have been like. Then, many months later, when Andrea would come for a visit, we'd hear her version of things. I usually preferred what we had invented for ourselves. Our own stories were really much more elaborate than what she would describe to us."

She turned to Griselda, then to Julieta. "Do you remember when we got the first package? The mailman brought it in October of 1925. I was fifteen then and my life was so ordinary and boring in comparison to Andrea's."

Mother began to reminisce about Andrea's departure from home in early 1925. "That was the year she went to live in San Antonio. A year earlier Consuelo and Tomás had gotten married. He got a job in the advertising department at *La Prensa* and they moved to San Antonio. Then a little while later, Andrea and Tía Florencia went to live with them. Andrea had just turned fifteen then but she was already pretty well-known here. Pepita Montemayor had chosen her as the lead dancer in every one of her programs. She had even selected her as her assistant and took her to Mexico City for additional training. You can imagine how disappointed Pepita was when Andrea told her she was leaving. 'But you don't have any contacts there.' Pepita had warned her. Still, Andrea thought her career stood a better chance of taking off there. And she was right. It did.

"In San Antonio she found a job as an usherette after school at the Teatro Zaragoza, a grand theater at that time. This allowed her to continue her classes and also to get to know the dance companies that performed there."

Mother paused a bit and Julieta picked up the story. "At the Teatro Zaragoza she discovered a whole new world. Right after she saw 'Los Amores de Ramona,' she decided to dedicate herself totally to the theater. That's also where she had her first contact with *zarzuelas* and *sainetes*, the short pieces from Spanish popular theater. One day she read an announcement in *La Prensa* about a *zarzuela* called 'La Señora Capitana.' She auditioned and of course had no trouble getting accepted into the chorus as a dancer. With that bit part she was on her way."

"That's true, but remember that she went completely against Consuelo's wishes," Griselda interrupted. "*'No te metas más en ese mundo'* Consuelo kept saying to her. In the end, though, Consuelo lost out and Andrea got her way."

As usual, mother quietly came to Andrea's defense. "With her earnings she signed up for voice lessons, and by 1927 she had started to work in operettas as well as in *zarzuelas*. I'm quite sure she had a small part in 'La Viuda Alegre' but I don't have a photograph of her in that role. *Más que nada*, she performed at the Teatro Hidalgo and at the Zendejas in plays written by Spanish playwrights and in a few works by some native Tejanos."

"How come she didn't stay in San Antonio?" Patricia asked.

"Well, in 1930 things got rough for the theater there. So Andrea and some of her friends decided to go West. They had heard that the Depression was not having a negative effect on the theater in Los Angeles in the same way that it was in Texas. On the way there, she performed in the Southwest—in Tucson and Santa Fe. Then she stayed in Los Angeles for quite a while. But by 1936 she was back in Texas touring through the small border towns: Brownsville, Rio Grande, Laredo, Eagle Pass, El Paso. She got as far south as Monterrey and Saltillo and eventually, she made it to New York. There she found the Spanish exiles very excited about the works of a young playwright. García Lorca. But I don't think she ever appeared in any of his works."

As usual, Griselda suddenly changed the direction of the story. "By then she was already involved with Tony Carducci. After they got married in '41, they went to live in St. Louis, Missouri, where Tony's parents were living. There, Andrea said 'bye-bye' to the theater forever."

Mother then ended the familiar narrative. "In 1938 Consuelo lost Tomás in a horrible car accident. Four years later it was her turn to join Andrea and Tony in St.Louis. Ever since then, they have all been together. But Andrea has told me that Consuelo has never asked her about her fifteen years as a performer. She's just pretended all those years didn't happen."

"Consuelo has always been very stubborn," Julieta concluded.

"Here the three of us kept close watch over everything Andrea did. And her own sister pretended those things didn't happen just 'cause she didn't approve of them. *Qué extraña!*"

Surprising even myself by changing the cues, I said quite firmly, "Andrea should never have given up the theater."

"I think Andrea has been very satisfied with her decision," mother replied. "She's never looked back. Once she reasoned it out with me. *'La rosa más bella dura poco.'* 'Every rose has its day,' she said. I have the impression that she was always happy while she performed. But after fifteen good adventurous years she wanted a stable life. Something she really hadn't ever experienced. *'No se puede repicar y andar en la procesión'* was how she summed up her decision. 'You can't serve two masters at the same time.' "

"I'm quite sure that if I had been in Andrea's shoes, I would never, never have given up the theater. Nor the dance," I insisted.

"Well, Nenita, you know what they say: *Cada quien cuenta de la feria según lo que ve en ella.* You see only what it is you want to see."

I knew I did not want to argue with Griselda; so, I looked for the photo of Andrea dressed as a *tehuana.* Turning the pages back to the year 1923, I heard the familiar mellifluous voice invite me to share the stage with her. The strains of "Zandunga" sounded faintly in the background and slowly we began to sway to its beat. As the music filled the room though, I could see that Andrea moved so much more lightly than I did, and slowly, slowly, I faded into the shadowy background so that the thirteen-year-old Andrea with the lacy white headdress could have center stage by herself, and she took it with full confidence. I closed the book and wondered what it would be like to finally meet this cameleon creature whose many days in the sun my mother had so carefully recorded. Shutting my eyes, I found that the lights on stage had dimmed but even then Andrea continued gliding, gliding so gently to the song that would sound in my head for a long, long time to come.

II

The 10th of July was marked in red on all our calendars. On that day Andrea would be arriving, not alone as we had first been told but accompanied by our cousin Consuelo. Tía Julieta had just informed us of the change of plans reminding us that this would be the first time since 1945 that both of them would be visiting us at the same time. On their previous visit the mood had been somber, for they had come to lay Tía Florencia to rest in the old cemetery next to the tomb of my grandmother, her only sister. To mark the change in tone for this visit, Memo—Julieta's husband—had purchased Mexican party-favors and at the train station he passed out handfuls of *serpentinas* and tin noisemakers to both adults and children.

In the distance we heard the train announce its arrival. A few minutes later, when it rumbled into the Missouri Pacific station, we waited for a sign to begin our welcome as passenger after passenger disembarked. Finally, a slender woman with short wavy hair, in a white shirtwaist stepped down and Griselda whispered, "Here they come." When a second figure appeared at the door of the pullman, Tío Memo gave a signal and we all sounded our noisemakers and sent the *serpentinas* spiraling through the air.

Tío Memo rushed to help Consuelo down the steps as billowing streamers wrapped themselves around her dark print rayon dress and her gray hair. The *serpentinas* looked even more dramatic against Andrea's dress and she quickly enhanced the effect by wrapping clusters of them around her neck. "*Bienvenidas!*" we shouted in unison. "Welcome!"

There were so many of us at the station it took a long time before my mother's turn came to introduce us to her cousins. Then, I felt uneasy facing the stranger in the clean-cut white dress. Andrea's smile did not exude the least bit of the flamboyance I had learned to associate with the figure of the picture book, and as she embraced me I felt my back stiffen. Consuelo, on the other hand, seemed instantly familiar; in her aging face I immediately recognized the solemn look of the ten-year old girl facing the camera of that unknown photographer in San Luis Potosí. I was glad she'd be the one riding home in the same car with us.

When we got home, Andrea's presence continued to disconcert me; so instead of participating in the noisy gathering, I merely observed the scene before me. She clearly delighted in the attention and chatted freely about the trip. "It felt like the old days, traveling by train," she was saying, "I loved rolling along all those miles of tracks." Her spontaneity was contagious to everyone. Except me, I thought. Then I noticed that Consuelo did not say anything either until there was a lull in the conversation and Griselda asked her what she thought of the trip.

"It was pretty much like Sis is describing it," she answered keeping to the role she must have played all of her life. I looked at her delicate figure, then decided to sit next to her on the floor, and as I inched myself towards her, she patted me on the back, then put her arm around my shoulders.

"Tell me about yourself," she whispered.

I whispered back, "I'll be a fifth-grader in September. But right now I'm preparing for my dance recital in Violeta Aguilera's class. It's next week. I'll be doing two solos and in three other numbers I'm one of the leading dancers."

I noticed she drew back a bit. "What kind of dancing do you do?"

"I'll be doing 'La Boda de Luis Alonso' by myself and with Cristina Ruiz and Becky Barrios, I'll be dancing two Mexican pieces, 'Tilingo Lindo' and 'Zandunga.' My other solo is my favorite. It's a Sevillana and I'll get to wear a white flamenco dress with bright red polka dots."

Consuelo looked away. Then she turned to me with her dark eyes. "Dancing may be okay for you now but you won't want to keep doing it later. It doesn't lead you anywhere. Take my word for it."

"That's what my teachers keep telling me. They say I spend too much time practicing. But I love it. I don't know what I'd do if I had to stop."

Just then Tía Julieta joined us. "We're breaking up the party," she said, "Memo and I are going to take Consuelo with us. After a few days we'll all trade visitors. For now Andrea will be staying here."

I felt a little disappointed, for I would rather have continued talking with Consuelo. But I decided to help my mother entertain Andrea as the three of us moved into the kitchen. Without saying a word, I brought out the blue album and placed it on the table. Andrea reached for it eagerly.

"Are these the photographs I sent your mother while I was on the road? *¡Qué gusto verlos!* You know, I don't have any of these pictures?"

She smiled as she turned the pages. "Tony's parents would have a fit if they saw them. Like Sis, they never approved of what I did. I'm not even sure what it is they objected to. But I've concluded that they didn't quite like the idea of anyone feeling comfortable and free in front of an audience. For them that's exhibitionism. But I don't know if that was really their objection since they've never wanted to discuss any of it." Finally her light-hearted laughter sounded familiar.

"Tell me, Andrea, do you ever feel sorry you gave up the theater?"

"Would you believe I never think about it?" she responded.

"I felt the stage was my calling and I truly enjoyed performing but once I gave all that up to marry Tony I was determined never to go back on my decision."

She kept perusing through the photographs as she continued talking. "When I first met Tony in New York, he was very good-looking and very intent on becoming a success. I confess I liked both qualities about him. He was always as outgoing as I was and we had a good time together. At the beginning we didn't think we had too many things in common. He'd been born in Southern Italy and had come to New York when he was nine. Then, gradually, we realized we shared more than we had first thought. Even though we were born in different countries, we were both raised here. We grew up rather poor but in very supportive and traditional Catholic families. Our first languages were very similar. And so was the way we looked at the world.

"His parents and I get along fairly well now in spite of their early objections to me. Consuelo had always been very strict about how we should conduct ourselves as a family, and I think it was because of this I was able to adapt to their sense of propriety fairly easily. But, she gets along with the Carducci's much better than I do. Tony's younger brother and sister even think of her as a great-aunt."

"How come she always looks so sad?"I asked.

"Sis is probably the most solemn person I know," Andrea responded, "but I don't think she's a sad person. She's had a tough life and she's learned to be very self-contained. We have so little in common. I'm sure we've both done a lot of thinking about this. At least I have. You see I was brought here as a baby and all the time I was growing up I always lived in the present. Consuelo, by contrast, had been very close to our grandparents and to all the relatives she left behind in San Luis Potosí. Already as a child she tended to live in her memories. And I didn't share those memories. She still talks about being uprooted and keeps the Carducci children entertained for hours with stories about her life as a child. Me, I never had the home she missed. So, I've always managed to live pretty fully in the present."

Andrea paused for a moment, looking straight ahead. "All through my teens, Consuelo compared everything she was experiencing to life as she remembered it in her solid city of stone. Once she even went back to live in San Luis Potosí but by then our grandparents had passed away. What she found there no longer corresponded to what she remembered. That all happened right after Tomás died. Fortunately she had a good life with him. But when he was killed in that accident, she went into a deep depression. And it was then that she decided to go back to San Luis. She and Mama set out together to their old home. But after only a year there they came back. When Mama had her heart attack seven years later, Consuelo became quite desolate. Now she didn't have anyone with whom she could share her memories and since I certainly was no consolation for her she took to the Carducci's instead. They became her family. She's even learned Italian better than I have. Everyone loves her, especially my kids, Antonietta and Franco."

While we were talking, mother had been preparing dinner. Suddenly, she came to join us at the table. "Andrea, do you realize you have not even mentioned the death of your father? For Consuelo that was a major blow. You were only three when he died. Too little to suffer any major consequences. But Consuelo was thirteen at the time, and she was much closer to him than to your mother. For a long time after he died, she would wake up screaming in the middle of the night. To make things worse, we had become so poor following my father's death in the revolution. Then, your father passed away only three years after we got here, and Consuelo and Griselda were forced to seek work. They were still children really but luckily the people at the fort took them in as housekeepers. Those *Americanas*

thought they were treating the two teen-agers like members of the family. But, you know, efforts like that never
really work out. All kinds of underlying messages somehow
come across. So, Consuelo always held herself aloof from
the Bristols.

"That family had an entirely different relationship with
you. From the first moment they met you, they took a strong
liking to you. Consuelo got their hand-me-downs but they
bought you lots of clothes. Later they even decided to pay
for your dancing classes. You were too little to see what was
going on there but Consuelo complained that they treated
you like a doll. I think that's the real reason why she objected to your performing. Oh, you might say she was jealous but I always thought it was more complicated than that."

Mother paused, then looked straight at Andrea. "Mrs.
Bristol and Mrs. Anderson not only doted on you but you
obviously cared a lot for them. And one has to give them
credit. They really did do a lot for you. Even after they
got transferred, the Bristols and the Andersons continued
to pay for your classes and your costumes. I think this was
very hard on Consuelo. People were always doing things for
you. But not for Consuelo."

Andrea became quiet for the first time since she arrived.

"Poor Sis," she finally said. "I do forget how different
our lives have been. What's strange about it all is that except
for the twelve years I was on the road we have actually lived
together all of our lives. First here, then in San Antonio,
and now in St. Louis. The big difference between us lies
in Consuelo's early years when I wasn't around yet. What
it boils down to is we grew up in different countries and in
different cultures. Odd, isn't it?"

"That's true," mother responded. *"Son las cosas de la
vida."* They both became silent then. Finally, mother said,
"Why don't you continue looking at your book? We spend
a lot of time with it. It's one of our favorite pastimes."

"No, wait," I quickly interjected as I ran to my room. "I have something to show you first."

Moments later I burst into the kitchen in my *tehuana* outfit.

"Great!"Andrea laughed, clapping as I entered. "Your headdress is quite a modern version compared to the one I had when I was your age. Mine was more elaborate. But it was so difficult to keep clean. And even harder to iron."

"I still would prefer to have an outfit exactly like the one you wore."

"What difference does it make?"Andrea retorted. "It's not what you wear that's important. What counts is not the costume but the dance. It's in the movement of your arms, the control of your torso, the limberness of your legs. That's what really counts. Just like in life. It's also very important to adapt to your surroundings. *Por desgracia* your outfit comes undone. What do you do then? Your castanets are stolen right before you go on stage? You must adapt to the situation on the spot. That's what makes the difference, not your appearance. *Tú sabes, el hábito no hace al monje.* Clothes don't make the person."

She reached out for me. "Nenita, what you are wearing is perfect. Now, tell me, tell me everything about your program."

"The recital is on Wednesday. But in a few minutes I'm going to a dress rehearsal. Right now I'd like for you to tell me everything you remember about these photos."

"Or want to remember." She smiled the familiar smile I had learned to admire in the photos. "Gosh, I haven't seen these pictures in such a long time. I can tell you're very intrigued with them though. But you know something? I'm really quite unattached to them. I suppose that's why I sent them to your mother."

"Mother calls this her memory book. I remember everything she's told me about your work. But now you can tell me the things I still don't know."

"Don't count on it. It sounds as if you all know more about the Andrea I was once than even I can remember."

It became obvious right away that Andrea really did not want to talk about the experiences which had so stirred my imagination. Disappointed, I closed the album and said I needed to get ready for my rehearsal.

"I'm taking the album to my room," I said, picking up the book.

As I walked down the hallway, I suddenly realized that regardless of what Andrea might now feel about her past life as a dancer, the images in the album could not be denied. I paused for a second, then smiled as Andrea's past flashed by me, on the walls and on the ceiling. One after another I saw the pictures I knew so well—the child in the shepherds' play, the young dancer in the chorus, the full-fledged actress in Lope de Vega's plays. Mother was right, I thought. She's always said that for us this album has taken on a life of its own. Because of her incredible patience in putting this book together, it will always be more than just a set of inanimate images, more than a record of Andrea's career. Mother has said it will always be the repository of our own dreams and aspirations, of the past as it was and as we would have liked for it to have been.

I set the album down on its usual shelf and skipped off to my class.

III

On the day of my recital, Consuelo came to stay with us and as soon as she arrived I knew we would pick up where we had left off four days before. The minute we were alone she pulled out from her purse a gold chain with a tiny medal of the *Virgen de Guadalupe* and handed it to me. "A gift for you on a special day," she said. Thanking her I slipped it over my head, then said hopefully, "Andrea told me you speak Italian very well."

"*Si. Mi piace molto parlare con tutta la famiglia di Tony.* It's very much like Spanish. The Carducci's have been very good to me and I felt that learning their language was such a small thing to do for them. Tony's parents remind me of my own relatives in San Luis Potosí. Grazia, his sister, is my dearest friend. *Mia cara amica. Uno di questi giorni andrò in Italia con lei. Capisce?* Did you understand what I said?"

"You said you were going to Italy. With someone, I think."

"*Con la sorella di Tony.* With Grazia, Tony's sister. I'd also like to have her visit San Luis Potosí with me."

"What's San Luis Potosí like? So far, we haven't gone there even though we're always talking about going."

"Oh, I guess you would find it a very tranquil place. I was very happy there once with my grandparents and my cousins. In spite of the revolution, they all decided to stay there when we came here. In those early years I missed them a lot. Then, much later, after Tomás died, I went back, hoping to retrace my steps and to recapture what I had left there. But by then Papá Enrique and Mamá Hortensia had died and my cousins and I had grown in different directions. At that point I felt I had no real family left. So back I went then to St.Louis to live with Andrea and Tony. Once there I became very involved with the Carducci's and their activities and now I'm quite comfortable with their ways. I'm even become a member of "Gli Figli d'Italia" and through the church I help out a lot in the San Giuseppe festivities. They're my family now. I hardly think about San Luis Potosí anymore although it's a beautiful city with many churches.

I'll always remember it as the home I left behind."

"Is Andrea as involved with the Italian community as you are?" I asked.

"Not really. Andrea has many friends all over the city. She's always going someplace with someone or other."

"You two are so different. Whenever I look at the old photographs of the two of you I can't help noticing she was always laughing. But you, you seemed so sad." I kept looking at her face, then paused and quickly blurted out. "Everyone says you didn't like for Andrea to be in the theater. Is that true?"

Consuelo's eyes narrowed for an instant. Then she became very quiet. After a while she shook her head. "No one has asked me that question before even though I've always known they all thought I objected to Andrea performing on stage. But that was never the issue. I really love the theater. When I was little, Papa would take me with him on the train to Mexico City. We'd go to the *teatro popular*, the opera, the *teatro de variedad*. We quit doing that right before we came here because of all the social turmoil. But by then I had learned to associate the lights of the city with the theater. When we first got here everything seemed so dark in comparison. And of course we were so poor we couldn't afford tickets for anything. Not that it mattered since nothing of the sort was happening here. Things changed a little after the war. In fact, Tomás and I went to hear Enrico Carruso at the Royal Opera House in 1921 when he stopped here on his way to Mexico City. That has always been a highlight for me. In St.Louis I used to go to the theater whenever I could afford it. No. No. It was never the theater in itself that I objected to."

Consuelo hesitated for a moment, then tapped my shoulder. "Before I go on, you should know that Andrea and I have gotten along very well ever since she and Tony invited me to live with them. We each know what we can talk about and what is best left unsaid. So what I'm going to tell you has no bearing on our present relationship."

She was about to measure her words. Then, inhaling deeply, she went on. "Andrea was spoiled by everyone when she was a child. I think that the woman I worked for—Mrs. Ernestine Bristol—added to the pattern that had already been set. Oh, they all meant well by their actions. Mama felt sorry for Andrea growing up as an orphan not knowing Papa like I had. Her teachers also treated her like something special. Then Mrs. Bristol messed her up even more. She never treated Andrea like a real person. I always thought she looked upon her as a cute little doll who could do unusual tricks. Take a bow, twirl to the left, give a good *zapateado*. Andrea loved to perform and she went along with all the requests."

"Wasn't she only five years old when she started her classes?"

"That's true. I knew then it was not her fault other people took advantage of her eagerness to please. I could also tell that the attention gave her the confidence she needed to continue getting better and better as a performer. But those experiences pushed her farther away from our reality. As I've already told you, we were extremely poor but Andrea never seemed connected to our circumstances. Someone was always taking care of her needs and she seemed to take that for granted. When she came to live with Tomás and me in San Antonio, she was obsessed with what she was doing and never contributed to the household. Her money went into voice lessons and clothes, into the social life that was more or less expected of young women like her. I soon learned not to expect anything from her, and I suppose I really resented that. But what bothered me most was the way she ignored Mama. Andrea simply took off to Los Angeles and all those other places, becoming more absorbed in her career. Months would go by without our hearing from her. I think she was much more in contact with your mother. Probably because Clarita doted on her accomplishments and made her feel important."

"There were so many other things I resented about her during those days. But it didn't do me any good to talk about them because she never seemed to be touched by anything that happened to Mama or me. When Tomás died she took off some days from work to come to the funeral but then she couldn't stay with me during the saddest period of my life. She had committments in New York, she said. After all I had done for her. That really hurt me. And throughout all this time I was quite convinced she was telling everyone I disapproved of her for being an actress and a dancer. And as I've just told you, that in itself was never the real reason I was so disillusioned with her."

"What if you had been in her shoes? Would you have done things in a different way?" I wondered.

"Who knows? Never, by the longest stretch of the imagination would I have gotten myself into the theater. So, it's almost impossible for me to answer that question."

"Consuelo, you two really had a problem. Mother says that anytime we think someone is doing something that hurts us we should talk things over right away. Did you and Andrea ever talk about all this?"

"You tell me what I could possibly have told her. She said she had obligations and it was obvious that she did. One time we had an argument over her lack of interest in the family. She insisted she had kept us informed about her life. Then she went to the drawer where she knew I kept her few letters and pulled them out as evidence of her communication with us. I became so angry I tore those letters to shreds. That of course made her furious. She picked up the pieces, tore them into smaller bits, then flushed them down the toilet. Since then, we have never exchanged a word about all those years."

"There's still something I don't understand. Today, on the day of my recital you've just given me this beautiful medal. Isn't it some kind of blessing for tonight? I had the impression you didn't want me to be a dancer either."

She smiled for the first time. "You've got the right idea about the medal. But you've jumped to conclusions about the other thing. I'm really not entitled to an opinion on what you do. But do you really want to continue dancing for the rest of your life?"

"I don't know. I only know I love my dancing so much I can't imagine not doing it. Every day I spend hours practicing.

It means so much more to me than making good grades in school. A part of me likes to study real hard but my great love is dancing."

"Well, you must do what is right for you. Tonight I'll be clapping for you as hard as I can. Who knows? You might even come to dance in St. Louis later if that's what you want. Do you ever think about visiting me?"

"Maybe I'll come just before you go to Italy. Then you'll have to take me with you."

"*D'accordo.* We must keep in touch."

As though to seal a pact, she reached out to hug me, and as before, I felt in the presence of someone I had known forever and ever. While she held me, I imagined the two of us on tour in Rome, chaperoned by Tony Carducci's sister. Everywhere we went I performed my favorite pieces and the faceless Carducci sister-in-law took photographs as fast as she could click the camera. In the distance a tiny figure of Andrea was pasting the pictures in a beautiful silver-covered album.

The image disappeared as mother made her announcement, "Lunch is ready. After you eat you'll have to take your nap so you can be all rested up for tonight. Everyone wants you to do very well."

"Guess what, Mamá?" I said. "Consuelo has just decided to book me at all the opera houses in Italy and she's
going to dance with me at the end of each concert while entire orchestras play 'Malagueña' for us."

"*Qué bueno*," mother laughed. "I better come along too,
to make sure I get lots of material for my second memory
book."

IV

That night, euphoric with all the congratulations and the
flowers and chocolates I received after the curtain call, I was
convinced that mother would indeed have lots of new material for her next book. Happy with this thought, I was
running back to the dressing room holding the red roses
that Consuelo had sent, when Andrea suddenly appeared
in front of me with her camera. "I want this to be a really
good picture," she said. "I've used up two rolls of film and
now I have only one picture left. I want a close-up this time.
Put your flowers down on the floor. Now pretend you're
dancing. Pose."

On cue I started playing the castanets while I danced
some steps from "La Boda de Luis Alonso." At the exact
moment when I held my arms above my head and crossed
my wrists, I saw Consuelo among the well-wishers coming
towards me. Tears were streaming down her face, and as
I looked at her I felt a profound connection to her. Why
is she crying I wondered. Aware that my smile had faded
I suddenly experienced a tremendous tiredness and confusion. Before I had a chance to compose myself, I looked
directly into Andrea's camera and at that instant she took
the picture.

V

I never saw that picture although I could well imagine what I looked like in it. Other things were also left to my imagination as the years passed by quickly without my seeing Andrea and Consuelo again. Life did not turn out to be as predictable as it had promised it might be during those happy hours we had spent looking at the many dramatic transformations that Andrea had experienced against so many odds. As much as I had thought during the summer of our first and only encounter that I'd be following in her footsteps, I wound up not pursuing a career in dance. Consuelo didn't make it to Rome either as she had aspired. But Andrea and Tony did.

Over the years I tried to maintain correspondance with both Andrea and Consuelo but it was mostly Consuelo who answered me. During the five years following their visit I kept them informed of my latest accomplishments by sending them glossy pictures with notations of the dates and places of the performances and the numbers I had danced.

All of that came to an end in my junior year in high school.

For reasons I have not yet deciphered, I allowed myself to be convinced that I should put away my dancing shoes and concentrate on my studies. My teachers, the school counselor and my mother all thought I needed to be making plans for life after graduation. With various options facing me I did not know anymore if I wanted to be a dancer "for the rest of my life" as they put it, and I decided that their advice about more practical avenues made sense after all. When I graduated from high school I finished at the top of my class and made it to college just as I and others had

expected of me. Every year, though, I made a point of visiting Violeta's best students to encourage them to stick with
their dancing, no matter how strongly others might discour-
age them from doing so.

Off and on I would compare my decision with that of
Cristina Ruiz and Becky Barrios. Cristina stayed with Violeta for many years, then opened up her own studio. Becky,
on the other hand, went to college and majored in dance,
much to her parents' consternation. She made it to New
York and occasionally sent me press releases about her work.
With those releases and clippings I gathered here and there,
I tried to keep a scrapbook of sorts about her many suc-
cesses. But compared to the one my mother had compiled
about Andrea's life as an artist, mine looked rather ordinary
and very much in keeping with my own generation's aspirations for fame in the big city, a fact which never entered into
Andrea's fun-filled peregrinations. Becky's hard-won suc-
cesses seemed meager when compared with what we all now
were exposed to through the media, and there was nothing unique about what she was doing. So my album looked
like hundreds of others that friends like me were pasting
together for their more adventuresome acquaintances. My
mother's album, by contrast, was simply one of a kind, in
keeping with Andrea's career which had been bold and extraordinary in its day.

For a short while, the blue album was actually mine.
When I graduated from high school my mother gave it to
me, and although I was very moved by her gesture, I also
had a slight suspicion she had passed it on to me as a token
of my having given up, on her strong advice, what had been
so precious to me for so long. At the dorm some of the
other students occasionally leafed through the album and
expressed surprise that I had a cousin who had been in theater so long ago. No one I knew then could say the same
thing. In fact, no one I know now can say it either.

As the years passed, I became even more aware of just how special Andrea's early experiences had been, and for her fifty-fifth birthday I decided she should finally be reunited with the images of her youth. At that time I considered my gesture to be most magnanimous; hence, when she called to acknowledge receipt of the album, I was surprised to sense that she was not particularly happy that I had given it to her. "It really belongs to your mother," she said.

"You can send it back to her if you'd like," I told her but when the album did not come back I figured she had decided to keep it after all.

Already then I was aware of how much I missed looking through its pages and recalling my own youthful aspirations. But I also reminded myself that what had been captured in those black and white images were her accomplishments and not mine. I had done the right thing in sending it to her I kept telling myself. At times, though, I wondered why I had not kept at least one of the photographs but again I convinced myself that they belonged, as a unit, with Andrea.

I tried not to have any further remorse about the matter, and in fact, for a long time I managed to erase the album's existence altogether from my memory. It all came back in May of last year, however. At that time Becky Barrios called me about an exhibit she was coordinating on women in dance. "Do you still have that marvelous album about your cousin which we found so inspiring when we were just starting out in Violeta Aguilera's class?" she inquired.

"I can come up with it," I reassured her.

Thus, I made my call to St. Louis.

Andrea was very happy to hear from me until I mentioned the reason for my call. Without the slightest hesitation she quickly said, "It's gone."

"What do you mean it's gone?"

"It's gone," she repeated. "It's been gone for a long time. About two years after you sent it, Antonietta was looking at it and left it on the kitchen table. Sis found it there and tore up all the pictures. Every one of them. Later she told me that she had shredded them into tiny pieces and put them in a bag. Then, she went down to the river's edge and sprinkled them into the water. As Sis described the scene I could see the little pieces of paper floating away like tiny white blossoms bobbing on the water."

"That's terrible," I barely whispered. "How did you feel at the time it happened?"

"I felt bad for your mother. You see, I always considered the album to be her own special way of expressing herself. I just sent her the photographs. But she was the one who arranged them in order in her picture book. Then she guarded the album like a relic. As far as I'm concerned I simply don't think back on the things that are a part of my past. For over thirty years I have not been a performer. You, however, acted as though it were only yesterday that I was still dancing and acting in the theater. You refused to accept that I truly had set those years aside. They no longer exist as far as I'm concerned."

"What can I say?" I almost apologized.

"Look, I don't know if this will make you feel better or not but after Sis tore up the pictures, we had our first real conversation about the tensions of those early years. Her resenting my absences, and my frustrations with her focus on the past. Her resoluteness. With all the links gone to the part of me that so disturbed her, we both discovered we could now really be as close as we should have been all those years. I simply accept her as she is. Deep inside, I suppose I've admired the fact that she has never swerved from her very strictly defined value system."

I still could not say anything.

"Look at it this way. Even though Sis had not known I had the album, her finding it served one purpose for which it might have existed in the first place."

"May I speak with Consuelo for a moment?"

Andrea hesitated for a few seconds, then said simply, "She's totally deaf now. Promise me that you won't write to her about this either. She seems quite happy in her own memories. No need to disturb still waters. Just let things be."

I paced the floor for quite a while after I hung up. Finally, I picked up the phone and called Becky. I would offer to help her with the exhibit in any way that I could. After all, there must be more than one way to put the pieces back together again. Unlike the time I was fifteen, on this occasion I knew what I had to do and I would not allow anyone to dissuade me from it. A clear-toned voice inside my head kept saying over and over, *"De una espina salta una flor.* Something good comes out of every bad turn." Yes, I would reconstruct my own blue album even if those memorable pictures had disappeared long ago, gliding gently down waters I did not yet know. Right before Becky picked up the phone, the strains of "Zandunga" once again filled my head. And shadowy figures in lacy white headdresses beckoned me to join them.

Amanda

¿Dónde está el niño que yo fui,
sigue dentro de mí o se fue?

...

¿Por qué anduvimos tanto tiempo
creciendo para separarnos?

Pablo Neruda

Los Lunas

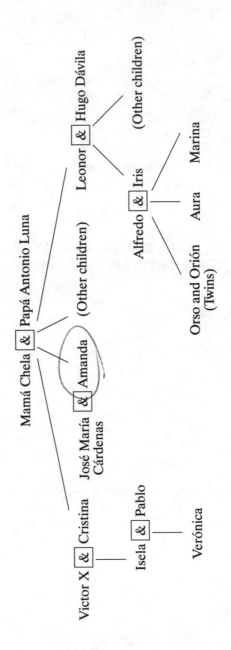

Amanda

I

Transformation was definitely her speciality, and out of georgettes, piques, peaux de soie, organzas, shantungs and laces she made exquisite gowns adorned with delicate opaline beadwork which she carefully touched up with the thinnest slivers of iridescent cording that one could find. At that time I was so captivated by Amanda's creations that often before I fell asleep, I would conjure up visions of her workroom where luminous whirls of *lentejuelas de conchanacar* would be dancing about, softly brushing against the swaying fabrics in various shapes and stages of completion. Then, amidst the colorful threads and irisdescent fabrics shimmering in a reassuring rhythm, she would get smaller and smaller until she was only the tiniest of gray dots among the colors and lights, and slowly, slowly, the uninterrupted gentle droning of the magical Singer sewing machine and her mocking, whispering voice would both vanish into a silent, solid darkness.

By day, whenever I had the opportunity I loved to sit next to her machine, observing her hands guiding the movement of the fabrics. I was so moved by what I saw that she soon grew to intimidate me and I almost never originated conversation. Therefore, our only communication for long stretches of time was my obvious fascination with the changes that transpired before my watchful eyes. Finally she would look up at me through her gold-rimmed glasses and ask "*¿Te gusta, muchacha?*"

In response to my nod she would proceed to tell me familiar details about the women who would be showing off her finished costumes at the Black and White Ball or at some other such event.

Rambling on with the reassurance of someone who has given considerable thought to everything she says, Amanda would then mesmerize me even further with her provocative gossip about the men and women who had come to our area many years before. Then, as she tied a thread here and added a touch there, I would feel compelled to ask her a question or two as my flimsy contribution to our lengthy conversation.

With most people I chatted freely but with Amanda I seldom talked since I had the distinct feeling by the time I was five or six that in addition to other apprehensions I had about her, she felt total indifference towards me. "How can she be so inquisitive?" I was positive she would be saying to herself even as I persisted with another question.

When she stopped talking to concentrate fully on what she was doing I would gaze directly at her, admiring how beautiful she looked. Waves of defeat would overtake me, for the self containment that she projected behind her austere appearance made me think she would never take notice of me, while I loved everything about her. I would follow the shape of her head from the central part of her dark auburn hair pulled down over her ears to the curves of the bun she wore at the nape of her long neck. Day in and day out she wore a gray shirtwaist with a narrow skirt and elbow-length sleeves which made her seem even taller than she was. The front had tiny stitched-down vertical pleats and a narrow deep pocket in which she sometimes tucked her eyeglasses. A row of straight pins with big plastic heads ran down the front of her neckline and a yellow measuring tape hung around her neck. Like the rest of the relatives she seemed reassuringly permanent in the uniform she had created for herself.

Her day lasted from seven in the morning until nine in the evening. During this time she could dash off in a matter of two or three days an elaborate wedding dress or a classically simple evening gown for someone's fifteen-year old party, which Verónica would then embroider. Her disposition did not require her to concentrate on any one outfit from start to finish and this allowed her to work on many at once. It also meant she had dresses everywhere, hanging from the edge of the doors, on a wall-to-wall bar suspended near the ceiling and on three or four tables where they would be carefully laid out.

Once or twice, she managed to make a hysterical bride late to her own wedding. In those hectic instances, Amanda would have the sobbing bride step inside her dress, then hold her breath while she sewed in the back zipper by hand. Somehow people did not seem to mind these occasional slip-ups, for they kept coming back, again and again, from Saltillo and Monterrey, from San Antonio and Corpus Christi, and a few even from far-off Dallas and Houston. Those mid-Texas socialites seem to enjoy practicing their very singular Spanish with Amanda who never once let on that she really did speak perfect English, and, only after they were gone, would she chuckle over her little joke with us.

As far as her other designs went, her initial basic dress pattern might be a direct copy from *Vogue* magazine or it could stem from someone's wildest fantasy. From then on, the creation was Amanda's and everyone of her clients trusted the final look to her own discretion. The svelte Club Campestre set from Monterrey and Nuevo Laredo would take her to Audrey Hepburn and Grace Kelly movies to point out the outfits they wanted, just as their mothers had done with Joan Crawford and Katherine Hepburn movies. Judging from their expressions as they pirouetted before their image in their commissioned artwork, she never failed their expectations except perhaps for that occasional zipper-less bride. She certainly never disappointed me as I sat in solemn and curious attention, peering into her face as I searched for some trace of how she had acquired her special powers.

For there was another aspect to Amanda which only we seemed to whisper about, in very low tones, and that was that Amanda was dabbling in herbs. Although none of us considered her a real *hechicera* or enchantress, we always had reservations about drinking or eating anything she gave us, and whereas no one ever saw the proverbial little fig-urines, we fully suspected she had them hidden somewhere, undoubtedly decked out as exact replicas of those who had ever crossed her in any way.

Among her few real friends were two old women who came to visit her by night, much to everyone's consterna-tion, for those two only needed one quick stolen look to convince you they were more than amateurs. Librada and Soledad were toothless old women swarthed in black or brown from head-to-toe and they carried their back sack filled with herbs and potions slung over their shoulder, just as *brujas* did in my books. They had a stare that seemed to go right through you, and you knew that no thought was secret from them if you let them look even once into your eyes.

One day, in the year when it rained without stopping for many days in a row and the puddles swelled up with more bubbles than usual, I found myself sitting alone in the screened-in porch admiring the sound of the fat rain-drops on the roof; suddenly I looked up to find Librada standing there in her dark brown shawl, softly knocking on the door.

"The lady has sent a message to your mother," she said while my heart thumped so loudly its noise scared me even further. I managed to tell her to wait there, by the door, while I went to call my mother. By the time mother came to check on the visitor, Librada was already inside, sitting on the couch, and since the message was that Amanda wanted mother to call one of her customers to relay some information, I was left alone with the old woman. I sat on the floor pretending to work on a jig-saw puzzle while I really observed Librada's every move. Suddenly she broke the silence asking me how old I was and when my next birthday would be. Before I could phrase any words, mother was back with a note for Amanda, and Librada was on her way. Sensing my tension mother suggested we go into the kitchen to make some good hot chocolate and to talk about what had just happened.

After I drank my cup, I came back to the porch, picked up one of my *Jack and Jill*'s and lay on the couch. Then, as I rearranged a cushion, my left arm slid on a slimy greenish-gray substance and I let out such a screech that mother was at my side in two seconds. Angry at her for having taken so long to come to my aid, I kept wiping my arm on the dress and screaming, "Look at what that *bruja* has done." She very, very slowly took off my dress and told me to go into the shower and to soap myself well. In the meantime she cleaned up the mess with newspapers and burned them outside by the old brick pond. As soon as I came out of the shower she puffed me up all over with her lavender-fragranced bath powder and for the rest of the afternoon we tried to figure out what the strange episode had meant. Nothing much happened to anyone in the family during the following wet days and mother insisted we forget the incident.

Only, I didn't forget it for a long time. On my next visit to Amanda's I described in detail what had happened. She dismissed the entire episode as though it weren't important, shrugging, "Poor Librada. Why are you blaming her for what happened to you?"

With that I went back to my silent observation, now sus-

pecting she too was part of a complex plot I couldn't figure out. Yet, instead of making me run, incidents like these
drew me more to her, for I distinctly sensed she was my only
link to other exciting possibilities which were not part of the
everyday world of the others. What they could be I wasn't
sure of but I was so convinced of the hidden powers in that
house that I always wore my scapular and made the sign of
the cross before I stepped inside.

After the rains stopped and the moon began to change
colors, I began to imagine a dramatic and eerie outfit which
I hoped Amanda would create for me. Without discussing it
with my sisters I made it more and more sinister and finally,
when the frogs stopped croaking, I built up enough nerve
to ask her about it. "Listen, Amanda, could you make me
the most beautiful outfit in the world? One that a witch
would give her favorite daughter? So horrible that it would
enchant everyone ... maybe black with wings on it like a
bat's."

She looked at me with surprise. "Why would you want
such a thing?"

"Cross my heart and hope to die, I really won't try to
scare anyone."

"*Pues, chulita*, I'm so busy right now, there's no way I
can agree to make you anything. One of these days, when
God decides to give me some time, I might consider it, but
until then, I'm not promising anyone anything."

And then I waited. Dog days came and went, and finally
when the white owl flew elsewhere I gave up on my request,
brooding over my having asked for something I should have
known would not be coming. Therefore the afternoon that
Verónica dropped off a note saying that *la señora* wanted to
see me that night because she had a surprise for me, I coolly
said I'd be there only if my mother said I could go.

II

All the time I waited to be let in, I was very aware that I had left my scapular at home. I knew this time that something very special was about to happen to me, since I could see even from out there that Amanda had finally made me my very special outfit. Mounted on a little-girl dress-dummy, a swaying black satin cape was awaiting my touch. It was ankle-length with braided frogs cradling tiny buttons down to the knee. On the inside of the neckline was a black fur trim. "Cat fur," she confessed, and it tickled my neck as she buttoned the cape on me. The puffy sleeves fitted very tightly around the wrist, and on the upper side of each wristband was attached a cat's paw which hung down to my knuckles. Below the collar, on the left side of the cape, was a small stuffed heart in burgundy-colored velveteen and, beneath the heart, she had sewn-in red translucent beads.

As she pulled the rounded ballooning hood on me, rows of stitched-down pleats made it fit close to the head. Black chicken feathers framed my face, almost down to my eyes. Between the appliques of feathers, tiny bones were strung which gently touched my cheeks. The bones came from the sparrows which the cats had killed out in the garden, she reassured me. She then suggested I walk around the room so she could take a good look at me.

As I moved, the cat's paws rubbed against my hands and the bones of the sparrows bounced like what I imagined snowflakes would feel like on my face. Then she slipped a necklace over my head that was so long it reached down to my waist. It too was made of bones of sparrows strung on the finest glittering black thread, with little bells inserted here and there. I raised my arms and danced around the room, and the bells sounded sweet and clear in the silence. I glided about the room, then noticed in the mirror that Librada was sitting in the next room, laughing under her breath. Without thinking, I walked up to her and asked what she thought of my cape.

"Nenita, you look like something out of this world. Did you notice I just blessed myself? It scares me to think of the effect you are going to have on so many. *¡Que Dios nos libre!*"

I looked at Librada eye-to-eye for the first time, then felt that the room was not big enough to hold all the emotion inside of me. So I put my arms around Amanda and kissed her two, three, four times, then dramatically announced that I was going to show this most beautiful of all creations to my mother. I rushed outside hoping not to see anyone on the street and since luck was to be my companion for a brief while, I made it home without encountering a soul. Pausing outside the door of the kitchen where I could hear voices I took a deep breath, knocked as loudly as I could and in one simultaneous swoop, opened the door and stepped inside, arms outstretched as feathers, bones and *cascabeles* fluttered in unison with my heart.

After the initial silence, my sisters started to cry almost hysterically, and while my father turned to comfort them, my mother came towards me with a face I had never seen on her before. She breathed deeply, then quietly said I must never wear that outfit again. Since her expression frightened me somewhat, I took off the cape, mumbling under my breath over and over how certain people couldn't see special powers no matter how much they might be staring them in the face.

I held the *bruja* cape in my hands, looking at the tiny holes pierced through the bones of sparrows, then felt the points of the nails on the cat's paws. As I fingered the beads under the heart I knew that on that very special night when the green lights of the fire flies were flickering more brightly than usual, on that calm transparent night of nights I would soon be sleeping in my own witch's daughter's cape.

III

Sometime after the Judases were all aflame and spirals of light were flying everywhere, I slowly opened my eyes to a full moon shining on my face. Instinctively my hand reached to my neck and I rubbed the back of my fingers gently against the cat's fur. I should go outside I thought. Then I slipped off the bed and tip-toed to the back door in search of that which was not inside.

For a long time I sat on a lawn chair, rocking myself against its back, all the while gazing at the moon and the familiar surroundings which glowed so luminously within the vast universe while out there in the darkness, the constant chirping of the crickets and the cicadas reiterated the reassuring permanence of everything around me. None of us is allowed to relish in powers like that for long though, and the vision of transcendence exploded in a scream as two hands grabbed me at the shoulders then shook me back and forth. "What are you doing out here? Didn't I tell you to take off that awful thing?"

Once again I looked at my mother in defiance but immediately sensed that she was apprehensive rather than angry and I knew it was hopeless to argue with her. Carefully I undid the tiny rounded black buttons from the soft, braided loops and took off the cape for what I felt would be the last time.

IV

Years passed, much faster than before, and I had little time left for dark brown-lavender puddles and fanciful white owls in the night. Nor did I see my cape after that lovely-but-so-sad, once-in-a-lifetime experience of perfection in the universe. In fact, I often wondered if I had not invented that episode as I invented many others in those endless days of exciting and unrestrained possibilities.

Actually, the memory of the cape was something I tried to flick away on those occasions when the past assumed the unpleasantness of an uninvited but persistent guest; yet, no matter how much I tried, the intrusions continued. They were especially bothersome one rainy Sunday afternoon when all the clocks had stopped working one after another as though they too had wanted to participate in the tedium of the moment. So as not to remain still, I mustered all the energy I could and decided to pass the hours by poking around in the boxes and old trunks in the store-room.

Nothing of interest seemed to be the order of the afternoon when suddenly I came upon something wrapped in yellowed tissue paper. As I unwrapped the package, I uttered a sigh of surprise on discovering that inside was the source of the disturbances I had been trying to avoid. I cried as I fingered all the details on the little cape, for it was as precious as it had been on the one day I had worn it many years before. Only the fur had stiffened somewhat from the dryness in the trunk.

Once again I marvelled at Amanda's gifts. The little black cape was so obviously an expression of genuine love that it seemed a shame it had been hidden for all those years. I carefully lifted the cape out of the trunk wondering why my mother had not burned it as she had threatened, yet knowing full well why she had not.

V

From then on I placed the little cape among my collection of few but very special possessions which accompanied me everywhere I went. I even had a stuffed dummy made, upon which I would arrange the cape in a central spot in every home I made. Over the years, the still-crisp little cape ripened in meaning, for I could not imagine anyone ever again taking the time to create anything as personal for me as Amanda had done when our worlds had coincided for a brief and joyous period in those splendid days of luscious white gardenias.

When the end came I could hardly bear it. It happened many years ago when the suitcase containing the little cape got lost en route on my first trip west. No one could understand why the loss of something as quaint as a black cape with chicken feathers, bones of sparrows and cat's paws could cause anyone to carry on in such a manner. Their lack of sympathy only increased my own awareness of what was gone, and for months after I first came to these foggy coastal shores I would wake up to *lentejuelas de conchanacar* whirling about in the darkness, just as they had done so long ago in that magical room in Amanda's house.

VI

Back home, Amanda is aging well, and although I

haven't seen her in years, lately I have been dreaming once again about the enchantment which her hands gave to everything they touched, especially when I was very tiny and to celebrate our birthdays, my father, she and I had a joint birthday party lasting three days. During this time, he would use bamboo sticks to make a skeletal frame for a kite, and then Amanda would take the frame and attach thin layers of marquisette to it with angel cords. In the late afternoon, my father would hold on to the cords, while I floated about on the kite above the shrubs and bushes; and it was all such fun. I cannot recall the exact year when those celebrations stopped, nor what we did with all those talismanic presents but I must remember to sort through all the trunks and boxes in my mother's storeroom the next time that I am home.

Filomena

My sisters, the birds, ye are greatly beholden to God for the element of the air.

St. Francis of Assisi

Filomena

I

Every year, in early November, the life of the dead assumed primary importance for Filomena and me, and in preparation for our commemoration, we were making our purchases at the *mercado*. All around us, pails of flowers— mostly *zempoalxochitles*, the color of the sun—were displayed, as one vendor after another tried to entice us with the same statement: *"¡Flores para los muertos! ¡Flores para los muertos!"* As we walked around, my arms formed a circle around the sweet-smelling clusters of flowers that Filomena had already picked out.

To get a little relief from the scent of the flowers, I turned my head upwards and saw that from the second floor of the *mercado,* sheets with large bold letters announced *"El 2 de noviembre—Día de los Muertos."* All over the signs, painted skeletons danced around a central figure who was draped over a chair with a scythe in his right hand. Years before, Filomena had told me his name—Mictlantecuhtli, the Lord of the Dead. *"Pobrecito Mictlantecuhtli,"* I thought to myself, "no one in school ever talks about you. Maybe they're all hiding from you." Looking at his bony figure, I whispered, "Ah, Mictlantecuhtli, you certainly are no stranger to Filomena and me."

I turned to Filomena to point out the skeletons on the sheets, then skipped the gesture. It was obvious she was through with her purchases and we were ready to go past the throng of celebrants choosing their offerings for the holiday. Awed with the beauty of the scene we would soon be leaving behind, I now took in one deep breath after another until I became intoxicated with the smell of the flowers. Like me, Filomena was holding the bouquets to her nose. Not wanting to break the spell of the moment, we walked in silence, content simply to be together.

Her house was only a few blocks from the marketplace, and as we approached it, I began to measure my steps by hers, giving her quick side glances. Today, as on most days, she had gathered her long dark hair at the nape of her neck with a black barrette. Her face was free of any make-up and she was wearing a gray rayon dress which came to her mid-calf. No doubt it was this simplicity of manner that gave her a certain agelessness and enigmatic wisdom. My mother, who had just turned forty, had once told me that she and Filomena were about the same age. This I found hard to comprehend, for they seemed so different from each other. My mother had a certain quickness of manner, while Filomena moved in slow steady paces—one, a volatile, unpredictable spirit, the other, deeply rooted and steadfast.

As we walked along, I kept thinking of the three people we'd soon be honoring: Alejandro, Nalberto and Martín. In the four years I had been helping Filomena with the commemoration, I had picked up a lot of disjointed details about Nalberto, her father, who had been killed in a battle at Zacatecas, a few months before she had been born. Even though I knew an assortment of facts about his life, my sense of Nalberto was vague, no doubt because of Filomena's own sense of her father. Perhaps more confusing for me was the fact that Filomena was already fifteen years older than her father had been when a *federal* had pierced his heart with a bullet. He looked so young in the only photograph she had of him that I kept imagining her as Nalberto's mother rather than his daughter.

In contrast to the indefiniteness that surrounded Nalberto, Martín had continued to maintain a presence in Filomena's life. They had been married in 1932, the year they settled in our area, and although she was always reticent about expressing her feelings verbally, she still had given me a sense of the undying love she felt for Martín. Often she described his fiery Pedro Armendáriz smile and his brawny body which heavy physical labor had made more sinewy. A deep sadness overtook her whenever she remembered the day he had been called to serve in the war, leaving her behind with the three children.

Every day she had gathered them in her little bedroom where she had set up an altar in honor of the *Virgen de San Juan de los Lagos*. Her *altarcito* had consisted only of a table with a small statue of the lovely dark-haired Virgin surrounded by her father's photograph and several snapshots of Martín. The altar had expanded, however, since she had added a small offering for every month Martín was gone. Then one day a young Marine had knocked on her door telling her that her husband had been wounded in Iwo Jima. A few days after that visit, she had quietly joined the legion of other women who mourned their loved ones with small black crosses on their windows.

Almost immediately she had enlarged her altar with a picture of the Sacred Heart of Mary. Her neighbors, knowing she found consolation through her sacred articles, had added two new pieces to her collection: a statue of the *Virgen de Guadalupe* and a tin *retablo* of the Holy Trinity, which she nailed to the wall, next to the images of the Virgin. In the evenings, after the children went to bed, she would spend hours kneeling in front of her altar, lighting and relighting candles, ridding herself of any accusations she might have made against God and the Virgin in the moments of initial grief. During the day as she cleaned houses she whispered away her sorrow: "and pray for us sinners, now and at the hour of our death. *Amén*."

Slowly she began to realize that she could not take care of the children by herself, for the work she was able to do never yielded a sufficient income. Bureaucratic stipulations overwhelmed her and she was unable to handle the required paperwork for her widow's pension. So, on the day she finally came to terms with what she perceived as her only solution, she gently informed the children about her decision. Alejandro would be boarded in a Catholic school and Lucila and Mateo would be sent for a short while to live with relatives in Michoacán. As soon as she resolved her finances, she'd send for the younger two.

From then on she worked at various chores at once but her primary job consisted of helping my mother take care of me. Needing to activate her quiescent maternal feelings, Filomena showered me with affection and I, sensing her deep love, began to view her as my second mother. By the time I was five I knew all about the various saints she admired, and on many occasions I attended novenas with her. On the day she was initiated into the Marian Sodality, I too became one of the *Hijitas* with the long white dresses and blue scapulars. Feeling that I was now connected to all the saints and martyrs who had ever lived and to the hundreds still to come, I began to listen with fascination to Filomena's endless references to an ever expanding pantheon of saints. I particularly enjoyed her descriptions of the religious festivals in which she participated every year when she and Alejandro went back to Michoacán to visit the other children.

Lucila and Mateo never came to visit Filomena, telling her they felt no need to leave the land of their ancestors where they were both quite happy. So Alejandro, Filomena and I spent more and more time together. During the summers and on holidays, Alejandro took a break from his tasks at boarding school and accompanied us to so many parish celebrations I soon began to feel like his littlest sister. I admired his gentle ways and considered him a good substitute for the brother I did not have.

When I was seven, Alejandro graduated from high school. Right away he got a job, hoping to reunite his brother and sister with his mother. By then, however, the seventeen-year old Lucila had a *novio* she did not want to leave behind; and Mateo, at fifteen, had clearly accepted his role as the youngest son in his aunt's family. Alejandro was truly disappointed at their decision, for it was unlikely he could join them in Uruapan, a place that had never been home for him. Filomena consoled Alejandro for the way things had turned out and affirmed that their lives were now to be spent in our city. Alejandro then wrote a long letter to his brother encouraging him to prepare himself scholastically so he could attend the university in Morelia. Then he dedicated himself to his role as breadwinner for his divided family. At that time he begged Filomena to take a rest while he provided for their needs. She agreed to remain at home but continued to take in ironing.

One afternoon while I was helping Filomena with her work, Alejandro walked in with three white wrought iron birdcages. We both admired their unusual workmanship, following him to the tiny screened-in porch in the back of the house where he hung them next to the geraniums. They remained empty for several weeks and finally Filomena suggested using them as planters for more flowers. As soon as she said this, Alejandro told her that within a week he would make sure she would never again be alone during his absence. Much to my pleasant surprise, in exactly two days he filled the cages with a variety of finches, canaries and orange-breasted lovebirds which added a joyful twittering to the house. Filomena gave a name to each of the birds and began to note the unique characteristics she found in each one. I had never seen her so enthusiasic before and she admitted that Alejandro had given her the best present she had ever received.

"I'll have to give you an even better present," he had remarked.

Alejandro was true to his word, and on a bright September morning when Filomena and I had just returned from Mass, he asked us to step out to the porch. There in a huge domed cage was a radiant green macaw with a crimson breast and a yellow poll. When she saw us she squawked, "*¡Loro! ¡Loro! ¡Loro!*" Then, as she walked along the dome of the cage gripping the roof with her large claws, she told us her name in a throaty voice: "¡Kika! ¡Kika!"

"Do you like her?"Alejandro asked with a glowing smile. "If you like her, she's yours."

"*Mira, nomás*," Filomena shook her head as if she could not take it all in.

"*Es tuya, Mamá*. She's yours," he repeated once again.

For a moment I was afraid Filomena was not going to accept Kika as she stood there with her arms crossed, shaking her head yet smiling as she inspected the parrot.

"Kika's an Amazona parrot from either the Yucatán or Central America," Alejandro explained. "I bought her from Mrs. Arzuela on the condition that I could take her back if you didn't like her."

Much to my relief, Filomena accepted Kika and since the *guacamaya* had been well trained by Mrs. Arzuela, the bird was allowed free rein of the house. During the day, Kika flew from room to room but she always returned to her favorite perch, a swing Alejandro had hitched onto a corner of the ceiling in the livingroom. At night, on her own she walked into her cage. Then Filomena would cover it with dark towels, letting Kika know it was time to go to sleep. In the mornings when Filomena removed the towels from all four cages, she was immediately greeted by the happy trills of the finches and canaries and Kika would add to the rituals with her own rasping sounds. Occasionally she also let out two or three whistles. The house which had been quiet for so many years had suddenly become alive again, thanks to Alejandro.

Unfortunately, Alejandro did not have enough time to enjoy the melodic pleasures he had brought to his home. Within six months after his graduation he was inducted into the service to fight the atheistic communists who, we were constantly reminded in school, wanted to take over the entire free world.

"Don't worry," Alejandro had said to his mother. "I'll be back. In the meantime you have Kika and the other birds to remind you of me. Every time you hear their singing, remember that my spirit will always speak to you through their songs."

And so Alejandro went away once again. Almost as soon as he left, Filomena taped a large map of Asia to the wall. In front of the map she placed a small statue of the *Santo Niño de Atocha*. The patron saint of travelers, she explained to me. And every night when she recited her prayers, she would look at the names of the strange-sounding places she heard pronounced on the radio and console herself with the thought that at least Alejandro might be fighting the heathens in some of those towns and villages whose names she herself did not try to articulate. In school we heard about the Yellow Peril that Alejandro had gone to fight, an enemy I tended to imagine as John Wayne riding over the eastern horizon with hordes of barbarians behind him, just as I had seen him do in "The Conqueror." As Filomena and I prayed for Alejandro, I would envision him as St. George slaying the dragon of the Mongolians. "Come home, Alejandro. Come home," I would repeat over and over after every prayer, hoping that when I opened my eyes, Alejandro would appear in the room with us.

Alejandro did not come back to us alive. Within a year of his departure he was sent home from Korea in a casket. I was so grief-stricken with his death and the denial of my supplications that for days I wept without stopping. All around me the neighbors shook their heads and said that fairness had betrayed herself when she had dealt with Filomena. Hearing this, I cried all the more, forcing my mother to keep me away from Filomena so that my lamentations would not add to her sorrow.

So, I only saw Filomena at the funeral where I was surprised that unlike the neighbors' strong reactions and my own uncontrollable sobbing, she seemed to respond to Alejandro's death with equanimity, for she only cried a little, both before and after the funeral, and then during the sounding of the taps. After that, she retired to her little room where once again she sat in front of her altar for long hours, praying for the souls of the three men in her family whose lives had been prematurely snuffed out in distant wars. This time Filomena's mourning period lasted through a month of solitary prayer and silent meditation.

At home, my mother recited stories to me about her own losses as a child and Tía Griselda told me about the way she had coped when her father had died when she was ten. "Every time I'd shut my eyes," she'd say, "I would see my father behind a bright streak of light. So I would sit for hours with my eyes closed, trying to get a glimpse of his face behind the light." Even as she spoke, Alejandro's young face would appear before me, covered by a golden aura, which in my mind I would try to push up, away from his face. Little Adriana would touch my shoulder, then whisper in her little baby's voice, "He is up there. You can't see him but he sees everything you do. Don't cry anymore. He's going to be with you again." The matter-of-fact tone in which she made her prediction consoled me immensely and I resolved to keep the memory of Alejandro alive.

When my mother thought it was proper for me to resume my old habit of spending the late afternoons with Filomena, I found that she had completely reassembled and expanded her altar. The table had been replaced with a wooden pedestal on which she had crowded in her various statues. Green votive glasses with perpetually lit candles were interspersed between the photographs, and on the wall above the altar she had hung a large tin mirror on which the flickering of the candles was repeated in soothing rhythms. Zacarías, her neighbor, had attached thick hooks into the ceiling above the altar. There she had hung her bird cages, seemingly to include the birds' warbles and the parrot's noisy voice as part of her offering. Moved by the beatific spirit of Filomena's simple heart, I took off my gold chain with the tiny medallion of the *Virgen de Guadalupe*, then placed it on the altar in front of Alejandro's picture. After that I joined her in prayer every afternoon while the birds chirped softly above us. As I knelt there I began to realize that my prayers were no longer murmurs of petition; instead, they had become statements of resolution: "Thy will be done on earth as it is in heaven."

II

As the end of October approached, Filomena was planning a trip to Michoacán to participate in the traditional Tarascan rituals of the Day of the Dead. Part of her pilgrimage would include the observances on the island of Janitzio and she wanted me to benefit from them also. My parents, who had never allowed me to travel with any of my friends even to near-by places, surprised me by being open to Filomena's suggestion. The experience might be a good spiritual cleansing for me, they reasoned, as they discussed the trip with the rest of the family. As a result of the conversations, Griselda finally agreed to go with us. So, on the 28th of October, Griselda, Filomena and I set out to Morelia on the all-night express offered by Tres Estrellas de Oro.

In Morelia we made connections to Uruapan, where Mateo, Lucila and her *novio* Mauricio met us. At first I felt a bit uncomfortable with Filomena's real children, knowing that in the last several years I had spent more time with her than they had. Both were very amiable, however, trying their best to put me at ease. "Lucila and I speak Spanish and English," Mateo had let me know. "So you can speak to us in either language."

"Let's speak in both," I suggested. "Sometimes in English and sometimes in Spanish. We can also use Tex-Mex." With that, we all laughed and settled down to the business of preparing the offerings we would be taking with us to Janitzio.

Rosa—Filomena's sister—and her husband had already taken care of the preliminary details. They proudly pointed to a five-foot cross made out of chickenwire which was ready to have the chrysanthemums mounted on it. Two days later, all the young people, including Rosa's and Arturo's three children, spent the morning in the adjoining field gathering the yellow flowers; later, we hooked them onto the cross with tiny wires. While we were busy with the cross, Filomena, Rosa and Griselda prepared the dishes we would be taking with us to the island. By mid-afternoon we were ready to set out in Arturo's truck to Pátzcuaro where we would be taking a small boat to the island.

Filomena and Griselda rode with Arturo while Lucila, Mateo and I sat in the bed of the truck holding on to the cross and other offerings. Along the way we took turns sprinkling water from a large bucket on the flowers. We also waved now and then to other families on the road who were as loaded down as we were.

"Alejandro would love all this," Lucila sighed. "He relished ceremonies. From the time we were very small, Mamá passed on to us a sense of ritual. Alejandro picked it up even more than I did. He loved getting dressed up in white during the month of May when he and all the other kids in the neighborhood would go to offer flowers to the virgin." She looked into the distance, then repeated, "Alejandro loved ceremony."

Mateo must have noticed that I had gotten very quiet, for he suddenly asked me what single memory of his brother stood out the most for me. After a pause I described the day when Alejandro had brought Kika home to complete the household of birds. "The birds have now multiplied," I explained, "so that every time there's a new batch I realize that Alejandro's music will be with us forever. He gave your mother the perfect gift."

After a while Mateo said he was tired of only good memories. "Let's face it," he said, "Alejandro was mother's favorite and that's why she kept him with her."

"I used to get very jealous about that too," Lucila admitted, "but sometime in the last three years I realized that she really did want us all together. She just didn't have the slightest notion of how to go about supporting us. I think Mamá assumed we would all come together again at some point. But it just didn't work out that way. Or at least you and I wound up messing up her plan."

"*No. No. No.* We really should have all come back here together," Mateo insisted.

"Once Papi died, Mamá would not have left him back there all alone. Now, you know she'll stay there forever. She's got to take care of both Papi's and Alejandro's graves."

"At least we're all here now, Nenita," he patted my cheek just as Arturo knocked on the back window to let us know we had arrived in Pátzcuaro.

Before heading for the lake he whirled us through the town, stopping at the Zócalo where I was amazed at the size of the colonial plaza and the activity already underway for the big festivities. When we finally got to the lake, many small boats were setting out, just as a dozen or so Tarascan fishermen with their huge butterfly nets were riding in with the tide. Already I was beginning to feel more at peace than I had ever felt before.

"You're staying with our friends in Pátzcuaro tonight," Arturo told Griselda and me. "And tomorrow you're being taken across the lake to Janitzio." Then he turned to Filomena, "Tomorrow you'll have to leave by three o'clock. The lake will be full of boats by dusk."

The next day we were at the shores of Lake Pátzcuaro by two thirty, loaded down with all the offerings we were taking. The boatman, an experienced navigator of the lake, was not at all surprised with our cargo. Compared to other loads he had carried to Janitzio in other years, he thought ours was rather light. His small boat was built in such a way that the cross could easily go in an upright position in the middle section. Filomena, Griselda and I rode in the prow and the others in the stern. By three o'clock we were on our way, gliding on the tranquil waters of the lake. Already by then, other small craft like ours dotted the view clear to the horizon.

"I'm really on a pilgrimage," I thought to myself, and with the waters lapping the side of the boat, I gently closed my eyes promising myself I would accept whatever happened. Opening them a few seconds later, I saw slightly ahead of us a small crew of fishermen with giant butterfly nets gracefully dipping into the placid water for the white fish that had made the lake famous. Watching the fishermen line up their boats in a row while they dipped to the right, then to the left, I felt I was entering a state of blissful surrender. My parents had been right; I was definitely undergoing a spiritual cleansing. While in this peaceful state I glanced first at Filomena, then at Griselda and I realized that they too were in a sublime mood.

As we got closer to Janitzio we saw hundreds of pilgrims already milling around at the highest point of the island, where the cemetery was located. Griselda pointed to the terraced slopes we'd have to climb to reach the top, then sighed, looking at the steep stairway. "Don't worry," Filomena reassured her. It would be worth the effort. She promised that in the morning, after we finished with the ceremony, we could continue farther up the steps to the balcony where we would have a spectacular view. In the meantime we followed her as she made her way through the multitude of people heading towards the cemetery with their offerings.

Inching our way through the crowds, we finally located the spot where Arturo's father was buried, knowing it was the only grave we could rightfully claim. First Mateo dug a small hole at the head of the grave, where we immediately buried the stem of the cross. Upright on the grave we placed about a dozen tall candles while Lucila arranged vases full of chrysanthemums here and there along the edges of the grave. The rest of us scattered yellow petals on the mound itself, where we then placed our photographs. When we were finished, Griselda rolled out a long cloth alongside the grave and Filomena gave each of us a small cushion.

As the evening wore on we took turns praying the rosary together, then relaxing, watching the people closest to us. All around us, crosses sheathed in golden blossoms let out a gentle fragrance and the glow of the candles added a sense of splendor against the darkness. Then, as the night emerged, the dewy wetness in the air became saturated with the pungent aroma of the flowers and the candles, and a sense of peace seemed to envelop the entire place.

After a while Filomena began to express the doubts we had each secretly started to feel. "None of them is buried here," she whispered. What if their spirits could not make their way back here as we believed they would? In the end,

however, the joyous scene aroused our faith and we set aside
our doubts, opening our baskets, and placing the food on
top of the grave. Lucila poured water into glasses and hot
chocolate into ceramic cups for our guests. Out of another
basket we took out our own food and ate, keeping conversation to a minimun, and, although I was sure the others were
as tired as I was, none of us lay down to sleep.

As the first light of day streaked the sky, the Indian flutes
began to sound here and there throughout the cemetery.
Their high monotones calling the spirits home dissipated
any misgivings we ever had about our loved ones. I shut
my eyes tightly, envisioning Alejandro smiling at me, with
Kika perched on his shoulder. Then, just as quickly as he
had appeared, his face was covered by a blaze of light. In
the distance I could hear the chirping of the birds getting
louder as he and Kika were suddenly absorbed by the sun.
"I saw him," I whispered to Filomena as she gently nodded
her head. Griselda, too, had an expression of bliss and even
Mateo was very quiet, staring out into the distance.

Lucila got up to embrace her mother and Filomena extended her hand to Mateo. "*Hijitos*, now more than ever,
I know I have to return to my little home up North. Why
don't you come back with me?"

Lucila put her head against her mother's shoulder, whispering that just as her mother felt she belonged in *el norte*,
so she and Mateo now had their home in this beautiful land
of perpetual springtime.

"Don't worry, Mamá. Everything is okay," Mateo murmured.

I kept looking at Filomena as we began to gather our
things. This is the happiest I've ever seen her, I thought.
Then she smiled at me, "Here we all find what we are looking for."

III

For the next three years, in contrast to the public communal festivities in Janitzio, Filomena held a private obser-
vance of the Day of the Dead; as her assistant I was her only
witness. We tried to keep our ceremonies as close as possi-
ble to those in Janitzio, even though we did not go into the
elaborate preparations that had taken place there. Here we
simply gathered the *zempoalxochitles* and other flowers at
the market on the eve of the holiday. Lucila, who was now
coming for yearly visits, was bringing us decorated bees-wax
candles which Filomena stored in the refrigerator until we
needed them. This was the one night she would leave the
bird room lit up so that Kika's screeches and the other nocturnal sounds could also form part of the offerings. I loved
our private ceremony but up to then, I had not been able
to recapture the spirit of the Indian celebration on the island nor the strong connection I had felt to Alejandro as
the sun broke out on that special morning of personal transcendence. Filomena reassured me that I would have that
experience again whenever I opened up to the gift of faith
as I had done in Janitzio.

Over the last three years, Filomena's birds had multiplied many times over and her small house had become a
music box of magnificent proportions, especially in the early
morning and at sunset. The daily concerts could be heard
blocks away but no one ever complained about Filomena's
happy birds. In fact, the other children from the neighborhood had started to flock to the house they were now calling "la Pajarera Blanca, the white home of the birds." At
first, five or six children had gathered on the sidewalk at
dusk as the birds warbled away. Then more youngsters be-

gan to huddle together. One day Filomena discovered close to twenty children mingling outside, delightedly listening to her birds. "If you promise to be quiet, I'll let you come in," she had cautioned the children who then tiptoed into her house in hushed whispers.

In her cage, Kika squeaked with excitement at the visitors. As if they could sense the pleasure the children were getting from their song, the birds twittered ceaselessly in splendid synchronism. From then on, Filomena routinely invited the little friends into her home. Once inside the house, the children became enthralled with the incandescent lights and incense beckoning them to Filomena's altar. First, one or two youngsters were invited to pray with us; then, five or six joined in. Pretty soon, as many children as could be accommodated in the little room could be heard reciting Filomena's litanies in soft, repetitive sounds.

For the celebration we would be observing in a few hours Filomena had invited everyone who had been in her house within the last month. Who would come would depend on the neighbors' willingness to give parental permission. As far as I knew, most of the children observed the occasion strictly as All Souls Day, as I had done in the past, and their main ritual would consist of visiting the cemetery with their parents, who would lay a wreath on the grave of their own dear ones. Most of them had never participated in celebrations as joyous and elaborate as the one Filomena and I had been sharing for so long.

As we neared the house, we heard the sweet trills of the canaries and finches which now took up the entire back porch. Their harmonizing seemed to rise a tone or two as soon as we stepped into the house, and while we placed the flowers in the different containers already pre-arranged around the altar, Kika flew above us in anticipation of what was to follow.

By sundown we finished with the basic assembling; next,

we distributed the bread onto plates nestled here and there around the altar and then as darkness set in, we lit the candles which made the room take on a bright glow. In the back porch we lit the only lights in the house. Tonight we would not use any towels on the cages, for we hoped that as we pronounced our benediction our feathered friends would accompany us with their song.

Before long the children started to arrive.

First Rosita and Laura from next door appeared, bringing four white sugar skulls with our names written across the foreheads. Next, Pepe and his four brothers showed up, each bearing candleholders shaped like a tree of life, which immediately went upon the altar. Zacarías's son brought his flute made of bamboo and Micaela's daughters each carried a tambourine. My best friend Aura and her brothers gave Filomena miniatures of skeleton-musicians made of gesso and gayly painted in vivid colors. Patricia and Adriana brought a surprise especially for me: a small wooden cross which they had decorated with chrysanthemums to look like the crosses in Mexico I had described to them. Even Verónica joined us bringing exquisitely embroidered napkins to cover the bread. Before long, eighteen children were gathered in front of Filomena's shining altar.

With Kika perched on her shoulder, Filomena invited everyone to kneel. As she recited the prayers for the dead, Marcos began to play on his flute and the Miranda girls gently sounded the tambourines which elicited the birds into song. Pretty soon we were enveloped into one voice, as the incense of the candles and the perfumes of the *zempoalxochitles* floated around the room. As the different timbres and vapors merged above my head, I became entranced with the joyous reverence around me, and slowly, slowly, a dream-like image of Alejandro began to take shape in front of me. At that instant I thought the birds' song had reached perfection. Accompanying them, the flute resounded higher and higher filling the room; then the sounds and scents seemed to swirl their way out the window, taking the birds' trills with them up, up, up into the night. Suddenly Kika left Filomena's shoulder and perched herself on the altar. I looked at her red lores and her blue cheeks while she positioned herself for a night's sleep, and I knew that just a few seconds before, Alejandro had finally come home once again. Rejoicing I prayed, *"Amen! Amen! Amen!"*

IV

By coincidence, ten years later I was home on the day that Kika died of a sudden attack of pneumonia.

"Se murió la Kika anoche," Filomena told me when I came by unexpectedly in the late morning.

"How can that be? What happened?" Aware of how long Amazona parrots are supposed to live, I had assumed that Kika would be around for years and years. In shock I let Filomena guide me into the kitchen where Kika was laid out in a bright lacquered wooden chest from Olinalá. Filomena had lined the box with Kika's grains, then laid her sideways on top of her food.

My eyes filled with tears as I listened to the silence in the house and marvelled at how the other birds must be sensing the passing of their companion. The only sounds came from Filomena as she described her surprise at finding Kika on her back, her claws gripping the heavy air above her. Her first reaction had been to craddle Kika in her arms, and when she had finally accepted that her pet was dead, she had called a taxidermist in the hopes of giving her a new life. Now, quite resolutely she stated that her memories of her parrot would suffice. Kika's great bird nature had consisted precisely in her moving about from room to room, letting out her rasping screeches. *"Fue una buena compañera. A wonderfull present from my Alejandro."*

We took Kika's box to the back yard and buried her under a pecan tree. Then, as we were down on our knees patting down the mound, we began to hear the cooing of the finches. One by one the birds picked up the sounds. Suddenly they burst out into their usual song.

"How lovely! They're saying good-bye to their friend," Filomena commented very matter-of-factly. Then, she traced the sign of the cross on the loose dirt. *"Requiescat in pacem,"* she murmured.

V

For many hours Filomena and I conversed, reminiscing over the many memories we shared of Kika and of Alejandro. As we went over the old days, I felt somewhat reaffirmed in what I subconsciously had come to seek. Lately I had been feeling very uncomfortable in one of my first graduate classes at the university. A middle-aged professor-poet, already on his way to becoming one of the major voices in American letters, taught his literature class with a degree of cynicism that made me uncomfortable. His total rejection of spiritual epiphanies bothered other members of the class, as well, and so we had started to meet on our own to comment more freely on some of the writers we were reading. Even with our more open discussions in the small group, I still felt I was losing my old sense of identity. At times I even felt that many new images were being imprinted on me and that I had not even had the chance to approve or reject what was happening.

A few days before coming home I had paid a visit to the campus chapel where I had sat by myself in the front pew for a long time, staring at the statues on the strangely austere altar, unable to draw out the familiar consolation I sought. "Maybe I'm becoming a non-believer," I had thought to myself as I gathered my things, then headed down the lonely, narrow aisle, never to come back. Outside, the bright afternoon light only emphasized my sadness which I tried to overcome by recalling the many happy hours I had spent with Filomena and Kika and the neighborhood children who had come to our novenas. The contrast between the past and the present was so immense that I began to question whether things had really been the way I was remembering them. I knew then that I needed to go home.

Now, even Kika was gone. As I faced Filomena I suddenly began to have an uneasy feeling which soon seemed to take control of me. Perhaps the visit was not doing me much good after all.

"She's too accepting of everything that happens to her," I complained to my mother. "'Así lo quiere Dios' is always on her lips."

"That's true. But Filomena is truly one of the happiest people I know, in spite of all the blows life has given her," was my mother's response, adding to my emerging dissatisfaction with what I perceived as their lack of critical thinking.

When I left that weekend I was even more confused than when I had come. Kika's death saddened me tremendously, for she had been my direct link to the memory of Alejandro and to the saddest and the happiest moments of my childhood. I was also very disturbed with Filomena's resignation to the death of so many of her loved ones. How easily she seemed to have given up Kika. Perhaps she hadn't really cared deeply about her, after all. Nor about any of the people in her life. This might be the reason why she had been willing to part with her children so many years ago. Would she react the same way if I went away for good?

As a defense against my new confusion, I began to give myself full-heartedly to the ideas of writers I admired for asking the right questions about being and about giving meaning to one's life through action: Sartre, Camus, Sábato, Beckett. Still, I sensed that in the end their philosophical conclusion about the essence of life seemed so meaningless and absurd. How long could one really appreciate their principles? "At bottom, it's a decadent philosophy, isn't it? Their ideas strike me as the perspective of a world in agony," I commented to one of my favorite professors.

"You do need to question the position of those writers," she advised. "Here. I think you'll enjoy reading this little story. From what you've told me about yourself, I think you'll relate to it." She smiled as she handed me a copy of *Trois contes*. "Read 'Un cöeur simple.' 'A simple heart.' It's Flaubert's masterpiece. As you read it you'll see why I'm suggesting it to you."

"This story is about Filomena," I said to myself as I mulled over every word about the simple-hearted Félicitè and the great love she bore for her parrot Loulou whom she eventually transformed into her own image of God. Always physically and psychologically isolated, Félicitè lived through a state of loneliness that became more acute as she got older. Loulou then assumed a position of paramount importance in her life, leading Félicitè to conclude that the bird that people usually identified with the Holy Ghost had mistakenly been seen as a dove when in reality she had actually been a parrot. Convinced that Loulou was really an extension of the deity, Félicitè managed to transform her parrot into the image of God at the moment of her own death. As her spirit entered heaven in a mist of incense, Flaubert describes the parting of the clouds and the emergence of a large parrot which opened its wings to welcome

and embrace the soul of Félicitè. Touched, I closed the
book,
amazed that the cynical Flaubert had actually given such
credence to the faith of a simplehearted maid.

What answer I had found I was not really sure, but for
the moment I decided that I needed to put a halt to the
years of abstract thinking and to involve myself more with
tangible and communal action. For me these new interests
became personified in community activities. I found a real
sense of authenticity through new contacts in many different projects but it was in the community arts that I found my
most meaningful outlet. For a long time I participated in
colorful exhibits in the parks, poetry readings in community
centers, sales of folk crafts, coordination of children's folk-
loric dances. I felt that these activities connected me back
to the stimulating creativity of the people who had served
as my mentors as I was growing up, at the same time that
they satisfied my new needs to move away from an alienat-
ing individualism towards a public collectivism much more
in keeping with the experiences of my youth.

For many years these activities fulfilled me. Then one
day I came across a new folk art which caught me completely
off-guard. There, on a table underneath a blossoming mag-
nolia tree, I saw dozens of earrings made to resemble the
folk altars that many contemporary artists were assembling
and exhibiting in galleries and museums. As I approached
the table, I noticed that the artist-vendor was wearing a pair.
I stared at the leather-backed keychains on which she had
pasted a laminated holy card of *la Virgen de Guadalupe*.
Around the inch-square "altar," she had glued rhinestones,
interspersed with red and green glass beads to resemble the
lights around some village altars. Amazed at the creation,
I listened to the artist describe how she had sold two dozen
in just two hours. "But friends have been advising me never
to wear these in Mexico," she laughed. "They tell me that

people might get upset that I've taken their national symbol out of context."

"*Sabes*, I've never had any real objection to people wearing clothing that resembles the American flag," I quickly told her. "Somehow that seems pretty abstract to me. But I'll admit that the sight of your earrings really galls me. I find them to be very insensitive to the spiritual beliefs of the people in the *pueblos*. I have a dear friend who would probably feel pretty sad at seeing you make light of her deeply-felt respect for religious icons. It's terribly personal with her."

"Oh, no! *No entiendes*," she retorted."This is my way of showing respect for your friend's faith. I grew up in this sprawling metropolis." She spread her arms to emphasize her point. "So I never had any direct contact with the traditional religious sentiment that you are talking about. This is my way of giving tribute to that experience."

"I'll believe you," I smiled as I opened my purse. "How much are you asking for a pair?"

With the earrings in my purse I made my way through aisles of tables filled with folkwares. As I walked around, I ran my fingers over the smoothness of the laminated cover on the icon. "Now, why did I spend my money?"I thought. "I wonder what Filomena would think if I gave them to her?" Immediately I felt ashamed for even allowing the thought to pass through my mind, then concluded, "Only someone from this centerless city could have come up with these gaudy creations!"

I paused to look around me, at one colorful table after another. Wafts of sweet-smelling grass drifted about everywhere. At the far end of the park, a combo was blaring out its electrical instruments. As I made my way through the people's artwork, I looked up to see dozens of colorful balloons which had just been released. For a long time I watched the balloons moving upwards until they disappeared into the distant air.

As I stood there, I kept wondering if I would forever go from one crisis to another. How unlike Filomena who had stood firm in the face of real calamities. Perhaps some day I would once again draw some strength from the little *altarcitos* that I had known in my childhood.

On the way home, I stopped at a dimestore to buy some crayons. For hours that evening I drew a huge image of Kika as I remembered her: thick green feathers, yellow poll, blue cheeks and crimson breast. Satisfied, I ran my fingers over the waxen image several times, then folded up my drawing into a thick square. Cramming it into a glass jar, I was ready to put the lid on it when I remembered the earrings. "They will serve a purpose after all," I thought, as I dropped them in the jar and headed towards my car, then drove to a near-by eucalyptus grove.

The scents from the eucalyptus trees became more pungent as I drove further into the grove, looking for just the right spot. In front of me, the road curved precariously but I drove slowly, knowing that no one was behind me. Suddenly the light of the moon filtering through the branches lit the tallest tree up ahead and I knew I had found what I had been searching for. As I stepped out of the car, in the distance I heard an owl repeating the same sound over and over. What a contrast it made with the happy chirps of the birds that had been Filomena's and Kika's companions. The owl's song was supposed to announce an impending death, I remembered. I listened to the bird, recalling other sounds I had associated with Filomena. Suddenly, whispering voices came to me from among the trees.

"*¡Flores para los muertos! ¡Flores para los muertos!*"

The voices continued as I made a shallow hole beneath the tallest eucalyptus, where I buried the jar. Suddenly I thought I heard a loud screech like that of the white owl of my youth. Uncertain, I listened out there in the dark for a long time. But no. It had been only the brown barn owl after all. I stood up as the wind rustled through the branches and watched a lone lizard scurry up a tree.

As I headed to the car, a faint chant sounded behind me once again. "*¡Flores para los muertos! ¡Flores para los muertos!*" I did not look back.

Leonor

Mist-filled Moon
rising,
rising.
The odor of sea foam
meets the fog.
And Coyote out collecting
dream fragments along the shore.

Judith Ivaloo Volborth

Leonor

I

Leonor thought the lizards that scurried up and down the south wall of her house had been brought on by the flood. The house had always attracted the transparent creatures but in the last year they had proliferated to epidemic proportions. "That's all I need," she mumbled over and over, for just when she had finally gotten her garden back into shape, Orso's and Orión's room had caught fire. It had not been a costly fire as it had not spread to the rest of the house, but she had lost several boxes of old papers that were stored in the closet where the light had short-circuited. Still, the flames had badly damaged the south wall and parts of it had cindered through to the outside. When the fire had died down, Leonor and Aura and I had watched the lizards run through the glowing walls. To our amazement they had remained unscathed.

With the rebuilding of the wall the little reptiles seemed to be attracted to the fresh stucco and had started to multiply even faster than before. Fascinated with the lizards, Aura and I started a new game. First we'd poke at a few to make them change color; then we'd watch them disappear into the ferns along the wall. When they would come out of hiding we'd remain still until they had gotten accustomed to our presence; then, we'd quickly move in on them, grabbing as many as we could by their tails. Most of our captives wiggled themselves free but we always managed to clutch on to some. These would give a tiny squeak right before they'd instinctively free themselves by breaking off their tail; then they'd rush off into the ferns once again.

Budding adolescents, we used that silly game as an excuse to hold on to our childhood for a while longer; as a consequence, it also led to our first lizard collection. From the start neither Aura nor I were interested in preserving whole lizards, especially after our first catch dried up inside the milk bottle where we had stored them. We soon discovered we could keep the lizards alive if we punched tiny holes on the lids of jars, then fed them spiders, snails or scorpions. That finding did not pique our interest in the least; so, we decided instead to collect lizard tails. At first we simply kept them dried up in our jars but soon we got bored with our inaction and began to string the tails onto bamboo sticks with thin nylon thread, giggling as we alternated lizard tails with multicolored cotton strips. Eventually we hung the banners outside the windows in our room and chatted for hours while the tails and cotton pieces fluttered in the wind. Unlike our mothers, Leonor seemed amused with our decorations and even promised to introduce us soon to her own hideaway, her house of mirrors where all fantasies became attainable if one but set her doubts aside for a brief moment.

Without question, Leonor Luna was the most intriguing member of the family but had she not been Amanda's sister, I am sure I would never have been allowed any interaction with her. Even more important as far as I was concerned, she was Aura's grandmother and for the past three years I had spent part of each summer with Aura's family. In those days Aura was my best friend and since I felt she was practically an extension of myself, I had no qualms in claiming Leonor also as my grandmother. She encouraged this relationship, and referred often to the two of us as her "*Estrellitas*, her Little Sparkling Stars."

Leonor had two consuming interests—her garden and her cards. She had inherited the garden from her mother and her knowledge of the cards from her grandfather. To a great degree she earned her living from each, hosting social events in the garden for a fee and holding private readings in her reflectory.

Extremely outgoing, she also had a streak of the meditative and the ethereal in a way that differed from Filomena's strong orthodox leanings. Leonor's spirituality mystified me somewhat, for it did not seem to have any connnection to the other religious practices that I knew.

My own introduction to her special world began one evening when she caught Aura and me on our hands and knees looking for stray lizard tails. "Okay, you little reptiles. How many lizards have you deformed today?" asked as she shook us by our pigtails. Leave those little animals in peace and come help me out."

"The Osunas are having a big party here in a couple of days," she told us as we walked towards the terrace. "I've got just about everything under control but I thought you might like to help me make *luminarias*. Melchor is going to put *luminarias* all along the path that goes from the terrace to the gate at the bottom of the garden. I would also like to have him put a few on the path that leads to the river."

As she talked, she half-filled a small paper bag with sand from a box in the terrace, then placed a candle inside a glass holder, nestling it into the sand. "With all these *luminarias* Melchor is going to need assistance on Friday. Perhaps you can help him arrange them on the steps that afternoon. Then right before the guests arrive, he can light the candles."

"We'll help him," Aura offered, her eyes brightening. "It's going to be so beautiful."

"Good. I knew you'd do it," Leonor responded. "I also have a favor to ask of you. Would you mind putting a stop to your lizard tail collection? I think the cards have been giving me warnings lately."

"About our lizards?"I asked.

"No, not necessarily about them. But I just don't want us to send out bad signals. Lately, every time I've thrown the cards for myself I sense that something is wrong. First, I get the water signs, then the fire ones. Next come the wind cards and finally I see the earth in motion. Over and over I get the same pattern. This has gotten me thinking about the fury of the river as it went over the bank last year, destroying so much of my garden."

She looked at Aura. "I also wonder about the fire in your brothers' room and the way the lizards passed through the fire unharmed. Lately the *lagartijos* have been multiplying all out of proportion. It might be a good idea if you quit waving their tails in the breeze. You might be messing around with the spirit of the lizard. You know I have great respect for the Great Lacerta."

"But look, Leonor," I piped in, "you've already fixed up Orso's and Orión's room and your garden is even prettier than it was last year."

"*Yo sé, Estrellita*. I know. But I also have great faith in my cards."

"Maybe you could let them rest for a while," Aura offered.

"*Imposible, Estrellita*. My cards have served me well ever since Papá Antonio gave them to me all wrapped up in a purple silk cloth when I was thirteen. At that time, Amanda and I were the only ones left at home. Mamá Chela showed her how to read tea leaves and Papá Antonio passed on his knowledge of the cards to me. I've respected their advice since then."

"Do Amanda and your other brothers and sisters feel the same way about them?"I asked.

Leonor shrugged her shoulders. "I don't know. It does

not really matter what anyone else thinks. It was the tradition to pass on the knowledge to only one child in each generation. Papá Antonio's mother taught him when he too was thirteen, way back around 1840. He chose Tía Concha, his fifth child, to carry on the knowledge but she died in 1913. She was fifty-six and for some reason which I never understood she had not passed the knowledge on to any of her children. At that time Papá Antonio was already very old but he picked me as the one who would carry on the tradition. Over and over we went through the interpretations until he was convinced I understood the wisdom they reflected. Then, a year later he died. It was 1915 and he was eighty-seven. I don't think too many people knew then he was a *sabio*, since he did not do readings for others as I do."

"Ever since the lands changed hands, people knew Papá Antonio primarily as a politician. At that time his brothers decided to settle in the new town across the river, beyond the new boundary that had been imposed on our people. But he decided to stay here and fight it out with the outsiders. Of course he eventually lost that battle but he had made a point of staking his claim by building this house. He was a feisty old man, full of life. There was always music in the house and lots of political activity. When *la revolución* was about to break out, he and Mamá Chela were already in their eighties but they still hosted several fund-raisers for *los revolucionarios*. I was a little thing then but I was allowed to participate in the *fandangos*. Once, the musicians played until five in the morning, then took off into the street with all of us at the dance following behind, arm in arm. Another time we went across the bridge to the railroad station to greet Don Ricardo. After that, the *rinches* began to patrol the neighborhood. Day and night. But those Rangers knew whom they were dealing with. Papá Antonio was never arrested although lots of other supporters of the revolution were. He used to say that the cards were on his side. I really thought he was invincible."

"What a character!" I chuckled

"Anyone who met him once never forgot him," Leonor continued looking at Aura. "That's why your grandfather spends all his time reading documents and newspapers and collecting photographs of Papá Antonio and others of his generation. He's putting quite a book together. Sometimes, though, I've wondered if we are doing the right thing. Here I am with my cards, looking into the future while Hugo is locked in his study with all his *papeleo* piecing the past together. If we don't watch out, the present is going to slip right by us. And speaking of the present, just look at all we've done while we've been talking. Dozens of *luminarias*. Paco Osuna is getting quite a treat even though he does not deserve it."

"How come?" Aura asked.

"*Ay, Estrellita*, Paco Osuna is the kind of *político* who strikes up deals with the old party even as he courts the reformers. '*Un peligroso*,' Papá Antonio would have called him. A dangerous one. This is one party I'm avoiding. Osuna is paying for the services and he's getting good ones but they do not include my presence."

"Does that mean we can't participate either?" Aura complained.

"Ah, but you two are going to do something much better. A thousand times better," Leonor emphasized. "While Osuna's party is going on, the three of us will be celebrating the solstice elsewhere in the house. You'll remember the night forever but you must do exactly as I tell you. Promise me?"

"Of course!" we both chimed in.

II

Aura and I had strict orders to rest in our room. Leonor could not have been more emphatic about the exact sequence we had to follow in preparation for our meeting with her. So after we helped Melchor with the *luminarias*, we washed our hair with the chamomile rinses Leonor had prepared for us, then sat on the porch next to our room letting the hot evening breeze dry it slowly. Later we brushed, then braided each other's hair into a single thick braid. By then our stomachs were begging for nourishment but Leonor had insisted on our fasting all evening.

Soon we heard the bells of the church sounding nine o'clock. Right away we put on our long white slips, then the white nylon dresses with gold trim at the neckline and wristbands—our leading angels outfits from the last First Communion Procession. Leonor had aroused our curiosity by assuring us that our meeting with her would have an even more profound effect on our lives, an idea we found excitingly sacrilegious. Finally, just before we left the room, we arranged a garland of gardenias on each other's head. As we tip-toed barefooted down the hall we could hear music in the terrace and for an instant I regretted I would not be attending the party. Instead, we made our way to the room that until now had remained locked for us.

We gave four gentle raps. Silence. We tapped again and looked at each other. This time we heard Leonor inviting us to enter. Holding hands, Aura and I went in together and found Leonor at the exact center of the room. She was sitting inside a circle that had been cut out at the point where two long tables criss-crossed forming an X. Mirrors lined the front and side walls of the room from floor to ceiling. In

back of Leonor, the wall was painted a deep turquoise and
on it hung an immense white wall candelabra. Shaped like
a tree, the candelabra also formed the outline of a pyramid
and inside translucent candleholders, flickering red candles
were dispersed on its branches. I was in awe as the lights,
reflecting on the mirrored walls, gave me the illusion of in-
finity.

My initial confusion increased when I smelled the per-
fume from the candles and the aroma of pine and *ocotillo*
floating from golden censers. I glanced quickly at the white
tree and the incense burners, then at the flickering candles.
Finally, I turned to look at Leonor. Behind her floating purple dress and veil she was almost unrecognizable. I stole a
quick glance at Aura in one of the mirrors and for a brief
instance I saw my own surprised look on her face.

"*Siéntense ustedes. Una a cada lado.*" With her hands,
Leonor invited us to sit down.

Aura took the crescent-shaped, backless chair on Leonor's right and I sat on an identical chair at her left. Leonor smiled at us but remained silent. Slowly she placed her
hands on a sandlewood box with increstations of mother-of-
pearl. Then she opened the box and from inside took out
a smaller one. The inner box contained a purple silk cloth
edged with silver and burgundy colored glass beads. Then
she unwrapped the cloth, first to the right, then to the left.
She murmured an incantation, then unwrapped the cloth
to the top and finally towards the bottom. Inside lay a deck
of brightly painted cards.

Leonor whispered instructions to us. "On this briefest
of nights, when the Northern Crown is at its brightest, I will
help to prepare you for the journey on which you are em-
barking. First one, and then the other." She signaled to
Aura to cut the deck, then to me. After the cards were well
mixed she spread them out. "*Es la cruz de Quetzalcóatl,*" she
explained. "*Y ahora para empezar.* Let us start now."

Hours passed by quickly as Aura and I took turns sitting in silence, listening to Leonor guide us through the journey of our lives. "Think carefully about the questions you want to have answered," she advised. "Without the proper question you cannot arrive at the answer you need. Wording the question is your most important challenge."

Leonor conversed with Aura for a long time, and once or twice I saw her wince as she read her cards. When my turn came my questions were very similar to Aura's; yet it was clear that our lives would be taking very different paths. Leonor said my journey would be closely connected to the Enchantress. Aura's path, on the other hand, would be linked to that of Mother Earth and she would experience several changes of skin.

As bonded as we were at age twelve, it seemed unlikely our lives could take such separate paths but neither Aura nor I questioned Leonor's interpretations. Instead, we listened with fascination while she did her own reading without throwing the cards for herself. "*Lo mismo de siempre,*" she said. "It does not matter how often I do my reading. It's always the same. A motion of the earth will bring the house down but I will no longer be in it."

When the cards were back inside their many covers, Leonor asked us to stand up with our backs towards her. In the mirror I followed her movements. She took out a pair of sissors from a small lacquered flat box. The sissors snipped, then snipped again. My head felt very light and I quickly turned around to see her wrapping our long braids in two separate purple silk scarves. Before we had a chance to react, Leonor began to explain her action.

"Just as the little lizards effortlessly develop new tails, so, too, your hair will soon grow long again. My garden suffered the consequences of the flood; yet now, a year later, it is more beautiful than before. Like it, your hair will become thicker and more beautiful. And while the cutting of

your hair commemorates a new phase in your life, let it also
serve as a reminder that transformations constantly regen-
erate our life. Remember that nothing is ever truly lost.
Whatever disappears or dies simply becomes tranformed
into something new. With this guidance, you can make your
way on your journey. Now it is time for you to go."

We walked back to our room in complete silence. Along
the hallway I was aware of the light in Hugo's study where
he was intensely writing the history of Papá Antonio's generation. And in the distance we could hear the band still
playing, for while we had been deep into ancient rituals,
Paco Osuna and his crowd had been heady into visions of
a new order which, in their estimation, would bring needed
progress to our area. The old order had in fact been renego-
tiated that night and under Leonor's and Hugo's own roof
without anyone being aware of what had been happening.
That night, however, Aura and I followed Leonor's instructions, and we slept with the deep peacefulness of the innocent.

III

By the time the public knew, several years later, what
had transpired, all the changes had been permanently arranged. The new *políticos* convinced the voters that urban
renewal would be a regeneration for the town. A new bridge
would be built in the long-range future, and as part of its
preparation, the old houses down by the river would be
bought up by the federal goverment. The youthful direc-
tors of the projects—college-educated and self-proclaimed
progressive visionaries—felt a twinge of regret at having to
raze a "historical section" but the order from above was for
change. Paco Osuna's son Michael had been selected as

the up-and-coming director for many of the federal projects even though he had only recently turned twenty-one.

At the time Michael was designated director of his first program, Aura and I were both eighteen. Already we were going our separate ways but we both attended a leadership training workshop which Michael was directing. Immediately he showed a personal interest in Aura, and in spite of the vehement protests from Leonor and Hugo, her parents did not attempt to block the courtship. Aura went out with Michael every night and dreamed only of having one baby after another. She was exactly the kind of girl he wanted and he pampered her with presents which made his claim on her obvious to everyone. Part of this claim was demonstrated in the quaint way he had of referring to her as his "Summer Breeze"; later, in fact, they named the first of their eight children Brisa, thereby inadvertently continuing with Leonor's desire to have her grandchildren named after the life forces that had so governed every phase of her life.

Leonor's dislike of Paco Osuna and his progeny had become so intense that she pretty much gave up on Aura, just as she had previously opted against teaching the ancient traditions to Aura's mother, Iris. Instead, she concentrated her attention on Aura's younger sister Marina who was just about to become a teenager. Marina seemed the perfect type for the honor. A fragile child with a wistful gaze in her eyes she seemed to possess special inner powers. Often, I wondered if Leonor had already initiated her into the ancient rituals but Marina's long braid made me doubt these suspicions. As I studied her actions, I soon noticed Marina was repeating many of the same patterns Aura and I had dreamed up for ourselves when we had been her age. One day Leonor even found a bamboo stick strung with dried-up lizard tails and pieces of rags hanging from Marina's bedroom window.

"*No, no, no.*"Leonor was telling her as I arrived. "No

more lizard tail flags blowing in the breeze. For years and
years my cards have been warning me about the wind and
the motion of the earth, and I don't want any provocations
to the great forces already at work."

I paused and wondered for the first time if Leonor actually tried to affect the future once it was predicted by her
cards. For the last six years her destiny had seemed so static.
Wasn't there something she could do to control the wind
and the movement of the earth which so threatened her?
Had she actually been phrasing the right questions to her
cards? All of a sudden I had so many questions of my own.
Would Leonor permit me to have any of the answers? Little did I know then that some of those answers were to be
found in Aura rather than in Leonor.

IV

Aura's and Michael Osuna's engagement was announced
at an elaborate party Paco Osuna threw for his first-born.
Although all the women in the Luna family had gotten married at San Agustín's and their reception had been held at
the family home, Aura's reception was to take place at a
ballroom at one of the hotels. Leonor considered this a
blessing, for the less she had to do with Paco Osuna and his
son, the better off she considered herself. In her eyes, the
changes Paco and Michael were overseeing "for the good
of the people" were merely steps that took the power out
of local hands and gave it to the *gabachos* up north. Papá
Antonio would have fought Paco with the same fury he had
shown to the outsiders in the 1850's. No doubt that for him
the *progresistas* would have been "a bunch of sell-outs."

Hugo Dávila had never exhibited the Luna's fervor for
their causes. In the more recent struggle, however, he tried

to contribute his share by recording the events of the last fifteen years. He was almost finished with his manuscript on Papá Antonio and he now dedicated himself to keeping extensive diaries in which he recorded how his generation had betrayed its responsibility to Papá Antonio's vision. Both Hugo and Leonor now kept very much to themselves, he in his study and she in her reflectory. Since Orso and Orión had left the house five years before, it had gotten extremely quiet around there. Now Aura would be leaving soon and of the grandchildren only Marina would remain at home. Iris and Alfredo, as usual, preferred to live in their ranch outside of town where their children visited them only sporadically. So, the wonderful white stuccoed house by the river no longer glowed with *luminarias* on its terraced garden and the music that had been so familar in the past was but an echo in the wind.

Michael and Paco Osuna quickly took advantage of the situation. Michael convinced Aura that everyone, including her, would be much better off if the house were soon sold to the government for demolition purposes. Sooner or later, the space would be needed for the custom and immigration offices included in the general plan for the next international bridge. The profits from the sale of the property would be greater now than if one waited until after the General Services Administration publicly announced the selection of the site for acquisition. Leonor and Hugo might even refuse to sell and then the property would be declared part of "eminent domain." Seeing the practical aspects in Michael's advice, Aura encouraged him in his vision but with one proviso—that Leonor and Hugo be allowed to stay in the house until it was absolutely necessary for construction of the bridge to begin. Michael quickly agreed. It would take at least ten years before the property would be needed and Leonor and Hugo were already getting on in years. In the meantime, though, papers would have to be signed for the transaction.

I could barely contain myself when I heard the plan from Michael and Aura. I turned to Michael first.

"Somehow you and your cohorts planned this manuever. Who is going to benefit from all this? I know, I know. 'The people will.' Is that in fact going to be the case? Or are certain contractors the ones who stand to reap huge profits?"

I stood very close to Aura. "And why are you consenting to treat Leonor and Hugo like this? It's bad enough that you want to tear the house down. Why not wait until they are both gone before any negotiations begin? You are destroying all that they value and you are laughing in their face to boot!"

"Come on, knock it off. We are being realistic," Aura insisted. "Leonor and Hugo do not need that big house any more. Just imagine what any repairs to the house will cost. It's obvious that Mamá and Papá will continue to live at the ranch. We're all out of the house now. Except for Marina."

"Just let things stay as they are for a few more years," I repeated.

"Don't you see we have to plan for the future?"Michael replied calmly. "We know two things for sure. The next bridge will be built in this vicinity although its exact location is not yet pinpointed. We also know that the custom houses will require lots of space. So will the immigration offices. The Luna property is ideal for that. And if all this is to happen we need to work with the local GSA specialists now. Obviously these negotiations cannot be made under the table. We must control our future. And that requires lots of planning."

"You are absolutely convinced you are right in this," I suddenly realized.

"Of course!"they replied at the same time.

Feeling powerless against such self assurance, I determined to break my ties with Aura and Michael. I wanted to protect Leonor in any way I could. Instinctively I rushed to the old house.

V

Instead of coming into the house through the main entrance I went to the back gate which led to the river and opened also into the bottom portion of the garden. In front and above me Leonor's garden stood in all its summer splendor. The bougainvilleas with their burgundy-colored flowers sprawled majestically against the stuccoed fence which ran parallel to the river. In the small tiled pond next to the fence, the water lillies swayed gently to the afternoon breeze. From my vantage point at the bottom of the brick stairs, I admired the giant ferns that bordered each of the three levels of the garden. At the east and west walls the crape myrtle looked like pink and white cotton candy.

As I went up the stairway I saw Leonor moving about on the terrace but it was not until I got closer that I was able to tell she was whacking at the lizards with a broom, her single waist-length gray braid spinning in the air as the lizards played hide and seek with her. Even though I had hoped to make my way up without her seeing me, she suddenly turned around and burst out laughing at my catching her in such a futile battle with the reptiles. Holding the broomstick upright with one hand, the other at her waist, she laughed and laughed.

"The reptiles have defeated me," she continued laughing. "But what a pleasure it is to see you, Estrellita. Come. Help me fight them. They've completely taken over."

"Don't hit them with the broom," I smiled as I stood next to her. "Grab their tail. Come on. Let's see who can gather the most tails."

For a few minutes we ran around pulling at the lizards'
tails. "Little monsters," I murmured under my breath."

Just then the window above the terrace opened and Marina popped her head out. Her lizard flags waved above her.
"What are you doing? It looks like you're chasing gila monsters."

"That's exactly what we're doing. Come join us."

In a few minutes Marina came down, her tousled short
hair bobbing in the air.

I gave Leonor a glance and she nodded her head know-
ingly.

"My time is up," she sighed. "It's Marina's turn now.
I'm counting on her to ask the right questions. I'm afraid I
didn't ask all the right ones myself."

"Come on, Marina. Let's go get them," I said, little
aware at that moment that Leonor's reading of her cards
had actually been accurate all along. In preparation for the
new bridge, the old Luna house and many others, including Filomena's small wooden home, were all eventually torn
down in the name of progress by the energetic new political
visionaries.

Esmeralda

I come from a long line of eloquent illiterates
whose history reveals what words don't say.

Lorna Dee Cervantes

Esmeralda

I

Esmeralda was the name they gave her, and for a long time no one seemed to care who she really might be. She had become a public figure of sorts, sitting for hours each day inside her rounded glass house. The crowds who routinely exchanged their coins for a new encounter with fantasy presumed she would be flattered by the exoticism they projected on her. Santiago Flores had been the first to refer to her as "*Esmeralda.*" In his daily flamboyant chronicle of local customs he had called attention to the "green-eyed beauty who greets the public at the Palace between one and six." For three days in a row he made reference to her, each time more exaggerated than before. "A beautiful jewel on display, one befitting the Museo de Oro which I had the pleasure of visiting on my recent trip to Bogotá." Finally, he had called her "*Una esmeralda brillante. ¡Esmeralda!* No name becomes her more." From then on, the public assumed a flattery that was more self-indulgent than well-intentioned towards the silent, bewildered young woman inside the glass enclosure. Throughout all the commotion she did not speak to anyone unless she was first persuaded that her reticence was a form of rudeness, a trait she tried to avoid at all cost.

II

When Verónica first started to work at the Palace Theater, before Santiago Flores had created the furor about
her, she had walked home by herself in the early evening.
Then the situation changed, and Amanda and Leonor had
wondered if I would pass by the box office after my dancing class so that Verónica could be accompanied on her way
home. After that, it was assumed I would meet her at the
theater every evening promptly at six.

Verónica was five years older than I was; but, of the two,
I had always moved about with more freedom. So, I was surprised she had gotten a job that required such direct contact
with a large public. She surprised me further by explaining
that the job had been her mother's idea. Since she was taking only morning classes to complete the credits she needed
to graduate, her mother had suggested that she now get a
full-time job in the afternoon. On the first day she looked
for work, she was immediately hired at the theater.

In a sense, Verónica had always been working. Six years
before, she had been brought to Leonor's house in a rather
mysterious manner. At that time, the twelve-year old girl
had appeared unannounced at the door, accompanied by
Isela—her mother—and her grandmother, Cristina Luna.
I was sent home as soon as they arrived, but from across
the street I had watched as the driver of the pick-up truck
brought in several suitcases. Soon after, he drove off. I
waited a while, then was about to head on home when the
truck pulled up again. This time Amanda stepped out and
hurried inside. The next day I found out that after Cristina
and Isela had consulted for a few hours with the other two
Luna women, Verónica had been left behind. From then on

she stayed with Leonor and Hugo, and each day after school she helped Amanda with her work.

From the beginning I sensed that Amanda made a special effort to insure I was never alone with her grand-niece. Several times after Verónica arrived, I also noticed that my mother and my aunt Zulema would cut off their conversation whenever any of us children were within hearing distance. So, even though I did not know anything about the new girl's background, I surmised there was something different about her and I withheld all my questions.

Verónica was soon under the tutelage of Amanda and Leonor. Amanda taught her to embroider with beads and in no time, Verónica assisted her aunt with most of her creations. Leonor too spent many hours teaching Verónica about the herbs and flowers in her garden and although the young visitor was not given to conversation she seemed to take in everything the aunts taught her. A little older than the rest of the children in the neighborhood, she was not paired off with anyone and spent most of her time alone, silently beading glass beads and sequins onto Amanda's garments.

Often Amanda's customers remarked on Verónica's beauty. *"Cara de ángel* with a personality to match," was how several of them described her. I did not disagree with their evaluation; still, I wondered if her desire to remain unobtrusive played a role in how they viewed her. Why, I wondered, did she feel she had to be so obliging? What most perplexed me during all those years of observation was that she never ever went home. Even more intriguing was the fact that she did not seem to have the slightest interest in going back to Alfredo's ranch where she had lived for so many years.

III

"Verde, que te quiero verde!" Orión recited in an insin-
uating tone, the minute Verónica and I got back from the
theater.

"Orión, quit that," Leonor told him.

At the same time Verónica murmured, "Orión, that's
mean. You have no idea how humiliated I am by what's
happened."

"Come on," Orión insisted. "Secretly you're enjoying
all the attention. You just don't want to admit it. This afternoon I passed by the theater and watched you for a while.
These two guys—the Mondragones—were trying to get a
smile out of you. But you were so high and mighty. Completely poker-faced. Come on, Ronnie, loosen up a bit.
They just thought you were pretty and wanted to catch your
eye. It was their way of complimenting you."

Verónica stiffened immediately. "I know who you mean
and they don't strike me as harmless." Then she began to
cry, softly at first, then uncontrollably.

"Ronnie, don't exaggerate. Why are you crying?" Orión
asked in disbelief.

"Orión, I've already told you to hush up. Please leave
the room immediately. I want to talk with Verónica in private."

As Orión was swaggering out of the room, I started to
go with him but Leonor called me back. "No, Nenita, you
don't have to leave. The three of us are going to have a long
discussion."

I looked at Leonor rather doubtfully but she signaled
for me to sit next to her. She then wove her fingers through

mine and embraced Verónica with her other arm. I waited for someone to say something, then gave Verónica an uncertain sideways glance. Relieved, I saw that she had gotten hold of herself and I concentrated my attention on Leonor's face.

"Nenita, even though you're only thirteen, you're really much older than your years. You've been surrounded by people who have shared their affection with you in many ways. I know, already you've had some unhappy experiences but you're really a strong girl. In many ways much stronger than my Aurita. In fact, I don't want the two of you to discuss the conversation we are about to have. You and I are finally going to help Verónica take control of an unpleasant situation. You see, for many years we have forced a silence on her. It really weighs on me. After so long I'm ready to assume responsibility for my own remoteness in the matter." Leonor took a deep breath. Then she turned to Verónica.

"Tomorrow you're not going back to work. I'll talk to the manager myself. I'm also going to give Santiago Flores a piece of my mind. *Lo siento*, Verónica. We should have made you quit your job as soon as the very first statement appeared in the paper. Like Orión just said, these men think they are doing women a favor by showering them with so-called compliments. *Piropos*. They think we should be grateful for the attention they give us whether we want it or not. It's really self-indulgence on their part."

She squeezed my hand. "Nenita, when Verónica was about your age, she had a problem. Something happened at Iris's and Alfredo's ranch where Verónica and her mother had been living for eight years."

Leonor paused. Then she looked at Verónica. "Let's see. Your father died in France in 1943. You were only five then. That's when you and your mother went to live at the ranch with Iris and Alfredo. Why don't you tell us what happened five years ago at the ranch? I've only heard other people's version of things. My sister Cristina has told me about it. Your mother, of course, always stuck up for you. So did Iris. That's why she sent her four children to live with Hugo and me shortly after you came." For a long time no one said anything. Then, Verónica inhaled deeply.

"His name was Omar," she began.

I looked at her as her eyes filled with tears once again.

"*Se llamaba Omar*," she repeated and looked straight out, trying to give shape to images she must have been struggling to forget in her recent past.

"He was from Sabinas Hidalgo, and he was only seventeen at the time. Slender. Like cinnamon tea with lemon and sugar. Sweet, very sweet. I didn't notice him at first but he made me take notice of him. Every night he would leave a present outside my window sill. The first time, he left something wrapped in newspaper. I opened it up and found a fresh prickly pear. The following morning I found another one, neatly sliced. It was ripe and sweet. That afternoon I was sitting on the porch. He came towards me. I didn't know who he was but then he extended his open hand, offering me half an orange and a slice of prickly pear. I smiled at him and accepted his gift. Then he disappeared without a word. The next morning I found a scarlet flower of the *ocotillo* on my sill. Then, a nocturnal blossom of the tall *saguaro*. Every night for two weeks he left a cactus flower.

"One morning I saw him heading to town with some of the other workers. I waited by the road for their return. Finally I saw the truck coming back. I pretended I was out for a stroll and waved as the truck passed by. Then, I turned back towards the gate. As I had hoped, he was standing there, waiting for me. I told him I also had a present for him, then I took off my locket and gave it to him. He opened it up, looked at the tiny picture inside, then read my name inscribed in the back of the locket. 'Ve-ró-ni-ca,' he said, almost to himself.

"Every night after that, I waited up for him by the window. He continued bringing me his usual presents and we would talk for about an hour, then he'd be on his way. One time I asked him to join me on the porch at dusk. He did, but Iris passed by and made him go away. 'You shouldn't be so friendly with the workers,' she said. Then she added, 'Besides, you're too young. People will start to talk.'

"From then on I wanted to be with Omar all the time. But we couldn't figure out where we could meet during the day without being seen. Then, one night as we were talking through the screen, I suggested that on the following night we wait until everyone was asleep and then meet on the porch. If we were very quiet no one would hear us.

"The next night we carried out our plan. Omar brought me another lovely cactus flower and we sat under the stars, smelling the pink jasmine, continuing to tell each other our life stories. We talked for a long time. Then I said I'd better go in. He put his arm around me and kissed me, softly, on my lips."

Verónica paused, then went on.

"I never found out where Alfredo came from that night nor how long he had been watching us. We had not heard him at all. But suddenly he was yanking at us, screaming obsenities. '*En mi casa no tolero puterías*,' he yelled at me. Then he slapped Omar over and over and threw him off the porch. By then all the lights in the house had gone on. There was a lot of confusion and all I remember is my mother taking me to her room. Alfredo was right behind us. 'If she's going to act that way with my workers, why should I wait my turn? Get your *huila*-daughter out of my house at once or from now on I'll take her anytime I want,' he shouted at my mother.

"*Pobre mamá.* She slammed the door behind us, then tried to calm me down. It was about midnight but she called

Mamá Cristina who sent someone to pick us up. We packed quickly. By the time the car arrived we were ready. I was terrified for Omar and wanted to see what had happened to him, but mother shoved me into the car ahead of her. Only when we were on our way out of the ranch did she begin to scold me. I was not trustworthy she kept saying. She'd have to figure out what to do with me. Now she'd have to get a job and think about where we were going to live. Mamá Cristina did not have room for two more people."

"You know the rest," she turned to Leonor. Mamá Cristina thought you might be able to keep me for a while."

"What happened to Omar?"I asked.

"I'm not sure. I never saw him again," Verónica replied. "I think Alfredo had him killed. Mother said Iris was unable to give her any definite information."

"Look, Verónica," Leonor said very seriously. "Alfredo may be given to bouts of violence but he'd never have anyone killed. I understand he called the *migra* and had Omar deported. He also threatened him with loss of his masculinity if he ever got in touch with you."

"How come Alfredo interfered in Verónica's life?" I asked. "She wasn't doing anything wrong."

Leonor sighed. "That's just the way it is," was all she said. A moment later she added, "My poor Iris." She refuses to leave Alfredo. At least she had the good sense to get the children out of the house."

"You got the five of us because of him."

"I have no complaints as far as that goes." Leonor touched Verónica's cheek to reassure her.

"It's nice of you to say that, Leonor. It makes me feel better. As a matter of fact, I think I won't quit my job. I'm really being a big baby reacting to harmless comments like I have. Please don't call Santiago Flores either. I'll be able to handle things from now on."

"Are you sure?"

"Positive."

IV

The mystery around Verónica was gone. For the first time since I had met her I felt I no longer needed to be on my guard as we chatted on our way home together. Instead, I thought about the shame she must have felt, being exposed the way she had been, dragged from house to house. And for no reason at all. I was particularly preoccupied with the way she had lost Omar.

"Do you ever think about him?"

"All the time. But I'll never see him again. He was so different from Orión's and Orso's friends. They're always showing off, trying to outdo each other in everything. Omar was a gentle, giving person. It hurt me so much every time I thought about the way Alfredo hit him. Even now it hurts me. Some day I hope to meet someone else like him. But who knows what will happen?"

"It sounds like you're never going to be rid of him. Filomena says Martín will always be with her. She says if you lose the person you love when you're still in love, you never get rid of him. That's kind of nice, isn't it? Your mother probably feels the same way about your father."

"Probably. I've never thought about it before."

Verónica got very quiet. Then she looked at me. "I wonder what happens to a person like Iris. Why does she stay with Alfredo? She couldn't possibly love him anymore. I have the impression he hits her too."

"Aura says he does. She hates her father. He got violent with each one of the kids. My father's not like that. He's very good with me. I love him a lot."

"You're lucky. I barely remember my father. After he died, I used to pretend my teddy bear was my father. I always made him promise to watch over me. After the incident with Alfredo I realized I didn't have anyone to protect me. In the long run that was probably as bad as losing Omar, for it made me feel very vulnerable."

"So we'll all have to take care of you." I looked up and smiled at her. Then, I got very solemn. "But you have to protect yourself too. Especially if you feel as vulnerable as you say you do."

V

Violeta Aguilera had kept us rehearsing much later than usual. So when we were finally finished I did not even attempt to change out of my leotard but simply slipped on my pants and ran.

When I finally got to the ticket booth the person on the evening shift told me Verónica had already headed on home. "She'll probably be very glad to see you. Hurry," the woman said. "Hurry."

I followed our usual path. When I turned the third corner I spotted Verónica about two blocks ahead. I ran up one block, then noticed that a white Chevy with big wings was inching along behind her. As I got closer I heard the two guys in the car catcalling her, "*¡Esmeralda! ¡Esmeralda!*" Verónica was pretending not to pay attention. I ran faster and got to her side as the two were getting out of the car.

"It's the same idiots Orión mentioned the other day," she whispered. "I told him they weren't harmless."

"Well, come on. Let's get out of here," I said just as one of the guys grabbed her and started to drag her to the car.

I hit him with my duffle bag and heard the cracking of the castanets against his ear. The other guy reached out for me but my dancer's foot hit him exactly at the spot where I had aimed at. He bent over, mumbling, "*Híjole.*" By then the first creep had pushed Verónica into the car. It was obvious they weren't concerned with me. The second one got in the car and they took off.

The street was deserted. I decided I was close enough to Leonor's to run there for help. When I burst in through the door I found Orso and Orión in the livingroom. "They took her. They took her," I said as I tried to catch my breath.

"What are you talking about?"

"Those guys you said you watched at the theater the other afternoon. Remember you told Verónica they were just trying to give her a compliment. Those guys." I pleaded with Orión. "They dragged her into a brand new white Chevy and zoomed off with her."

"*Los Mondragón.* Come on, Orso. Let's go get them."

As the twins took off, I started to pick up the phone.

"What are you doing?"

I turned and saw Leonor and Hugo. They had been in the dining room all the time.

"I'm going to report a kidnapping to the police."

"No," Hugo said. "The police won't do anything. Let the boys take care of business."

VI

The next day Santiago Flores's column contained the following cryptic statement: "Last night one of my favorite jewels was stolen, then shattered. The perpetrators of the crime were brought to justice but the damage they have

committed will be long-lasting. I am sorry for any negli-
gence on my part which may have contributed to what so
unexpectedly happened."

VII

For the next several weeks everyone took care of Verónica. Leonor meandered through her herbal patch, carefully
selecting sprigs of different properties to prepare into teas
and ointments. Blending either *yerba del oso* or *maravilla*
with baby oil, she'd pass the ointment on to Isela who would
rub it for hours into her daughter's skin, inducing her to
sleep profoundly for long stretches of time. After Verónica
woke up, Cristina would soak her in hot minted baths, mixed
with either *romerillo* or *pegapega*. Amanda insisted on stat-
ing simply that "Verónica had experienced a great fright."
To alleviate her from its effects, she ran palm leaves up and
down Verónica's entire body, then burned creosote in clay
urns next to her bed.

One Sunday morning I stopped by to see Leonor. As
we talked, she prepared a pot of steaming chamomile tea
and invited me to take it to Verónica. "Here are two cups.
One for you and one for her. You can visit with her for a
little while. I think it'll do her good to see you. All this time
she's only been seeing us old ladies. Three weeks ago she
was in a daze but all the massages and affection we've given
her have paid off. She needs to start living again. In fact,
Hugo thinks we should have a small dinner party soon. He's
going to invite one or two of his colleagues from the college.
It'll only be us, and Aura and Marina. You know the boys
have gone to stay at the ranch for a while. You are most
welcome to join us. *Ándale.* Go in there and perk her up a
bit. *Anímala.*"

VIII

Verónica was sitting on a rocking chair looking out the window, her long dark hair and tawny skin glistening with the sunlight. I was surprised she looked as well as she did and told her so.

"Ay, Nenita. Every day Mamá and Leonor, and Mamá Cristina and Amanda have scrubbed me up and down. They've wrung me out, smoked me through, sprayed me from head to toe with so many different perfumes and ointments that I feel like Cleopatra or Bathsheba. All day long they've all forced me to concentrate on the moment. On the present. In the beginning they made me tell them in detail what happened that night, first to one, then to the other. I cried and cried with each telling. And they cried with me. In fact, one afternoon Leonor said we were all going to cry together for the sorrows of all the women in the family. A wailing session she called it. *Lloronas, todas.* She went first and talked about Iris, her favorite child. She said there was nothing she could do to help Iris out except care for her children. Since all of us had experienced a run-in with Alfredo at one time or another we all could empathize with Iris. Later we prayed for her to face up to her situation and to do something about it.

"Then Mamá Cristina spoke. Everyone else seemed to be aware of her affair but for me all this was a revelation. Apparently a lot of people know her 'secret', but it's better if you don't mention this to anyone. It seems she was never married and my mother was born out of wedlock. She would only refer to the man she loved—my grandfather I guess—as Victor X. She said she was engaged to him, then he went away to fight in the war. She wouldn't tell me which war—the Revolution or the First World War. At any rate Victor X did come back the year before my mother was born. Mamá Cristina claims she was madly in love with him and had her first real passionate experience with him. He didn't bother to inform her he had gotten married to someone else until she told him she was pregnant. Later, when her condition was becoming obvious, her brothers sent her to one of the aunts in another city. For many years, though, she continued seeing Victor X. Then one day he took his other family up north and Mamá Cristina never heard from him again. When she came back, my mother was already six and Mamá Cristina did not try to explain her to anyone. The Luna brothers took care of the two for years and years. In fact, they are still supporting my grandmother.

"Mamá Cristina said she had no regrets for herself and she did not want any sympathy from us. But she did want us to lament for my mother. 'Isela,' she said, 'a child orphaned from a father who had not yet reached the Stygian shore.'

"My mother took her turn next. She started by emphasizing that wars are usually waged by men for dominance over other men. But their innocent victims turn out to be women and children. More specifically, she asked us to recall how one particular war, the Second World War, had left its mark on her, robbing her of a husband, a lover, a friend. Making her a widow and the mother of another fatherless child."

Verónica finally paused. "You know," she said, "I hadn't realized my mother felt as fragile and confused as she seemed to be that afternoon. It made me think I should help her somehow. But it also made me realize I don't ever want to get like her. Hearing her gave me the courage to take control of my own situation. So, when my turn came, I spoke in the name of all the women and girls who had experienced a sexual violation on the same day I did. On my own behalf, though, I insisted that the wailing stop. 'I do not want to become a victim,' I said and the others cried for me with relief. 'In the end, that is how we hoped you would feel,' Leonor said to me.

"Mamá Cristina raised her hands in triumph, saying we needed to switch moods altogether. It was time to describe sheer happiness, she said, 'even *picardía*, our own or someone else's.'

"This time she insisted on going first. She told us that a few years after Victor X had abandoned her she had thrown all caution to the wind and had gotten involved with someone else. To this day she considers herself in love with the same person. The confession seemed to take my aunts by surprise and they wanted more specific details. But she refused to tell us her lover's name and would only smile mischievously. 'But you never even go out,' Amanda told her. 'The only person you ever go out with is your *comadre* Celia Ortiz. Do you each have a secret lover somewhere? Oh, no! Don't tell me you're sharing a lover. Are you?' Mamá Cristina laughed so hard we completely forgot the sad mood we had worked so hard to get ourselves into. So then we told the good stories," Verónica paused. "The private ones," she finally said.

"Aren't you going to tell me any of them?" I asked, feeling I had been teased, then cheated of the bait.

"No. I'm not. We promised each other we wouldn't repeat those."

"Well, what was your own story?"

"You've already heard it. The one about Omar. But why am I the only one who gets to tell you both my own story and the stories I heard from the others? It's your turn to say something."

I paused for a moment.

Finally, I said, "Okay, I'm ready. This one is a salty story. First I have to ask you a few questions though. What's a *foca?*"

"A seal," Verónica replied rather puzzled.

"What's a *foco*?"

"A lightbulb."

"Right! But remember, you've just told me a *foca* is a seal. Let's just say a *foca* is a female seal and a *foco* is a male seal."

Verónica was giving me a dubious look.

"Remember, Verónica, you refused to tell me your good stories." I kept my eyes on her all the time I spoke.

"One morning Mrs. Foca was late to work. She waddled into her office half an hour late, swaying to her desk. All her friends noticed how clumsily she was moving but they pretended not to notice. Finally, when she was on her third cup of coffee her office mate turned to her.

" 'What's the matter, Foca? It looks like you didn't get much sleep last night.'

" 'That's right, Carmina. I was so tired when I got up this morning.'

" '*¡Caray!* Don't tell me you were working 'till late?'

" 'It wasn't that. You're not going to believe me *pero anoche me pasé la noche entera con el Foco prendido.*' "[1]

Verónica burst out laughing as she grabbed a pillow and hit me on the head with it. Then she put her arms around me, squeezing me tightly. "Nenita, it's been a long time since I've laughed like this."

---

[1]but last night I spent the entire night with the light on/with Mr. Foco turned on.

IX

Leonor explained that David Baca was Hugo's only colleague who could come for dinner on Wednesday.

David was new in town. A recent graduate from Houston, he was now associated with the program on international business at the local college. "David is teaching some business courses but his real love is *norteña* music. That's what really brought him here," Hugo said as he introduced the young man to us. "In his spare time he's making the rounds, recording small musical groups on both sides of the border."

"Do you play a musical instrument yourself, David?" Leonor asked as we sat down to eat.

"Just the guitar. I like to sing the old songs and to strum along as I go."

David turned to Verónica. "What about you? Do you like music?"

"All kinds," she said. "But I don't sing or play an instrument."

"Verónica is an artist of a different sort," Leonor quickly chimed in. "Her embroidery is matched only by my sister's. And there's no one who's better at it than my sister Amanda."

"Will you show me some of your work?" David asked.

It was obvious that throughout dinner, with subtle coaching from Hugo and Leonor, David made special efforts to involve Verónica in the conversation. Later, as he was about to leave, he thanked Hugo and Leonor for the invitation. "It's the first time I've had a chance to meet a local family," he said. Then, he added, "I think your niece Verónica is quite lovely."

"Well, David, why don't you ask her to accompany you the next time you go listen to music?" Hugo encouraged him, "I'm sure she'd love to join you. By the way, Flaco Jiménez will be in town tomorrow. Why don't you two take in his concert?"

X

David and Verónica went out every night after that. Since I was busy with school and dancing classes in the afternoons and Verónica was out in the evenings with David, several weeks passed by without our seeing each other. It was not until almost a month later, when Leonor invited me to join the entire family for a *merienda* in the garden that I got to see Verónica. At first I thought she looked quite tired but soon she was all smiles as Leonor said Isela had an announcement to make. The following week, Isela stated, Verónica and David would be getting married in a small, private ceremony; after that, they would be going to Acapulco for a brief honeymoon.

The announcement did not come as a surprise, and everyone managed to look cheerful and to wish the couple well. When I finally got a chance to get close to Verónica, I asked her outright, "How do you feel about all this?"

"I'd like to think I'm happy," she replied.

XI

When the baby was born, Leonor claimed that Verónica had been lucky to have had such a healthy premature baby.

"A bouncing six and a quarter-pounder," she told me when I went to see Verónica at the hospital.

"Let's go take a look at her," David suggested as he, Leonor and I headed to the nursery. "See if you can pick her out."

"That might get you into trouble," Leonor advised. Then she pointed to the infant in the third crib. "There she is. Verónica's little Destino."

"Is that going to be her name?" I asked in surprise.

"Verónica wants to name her Destino Dulce," Leonor chuckled.

"She's pretty set on calling her that. A girl named Destiny," David smiled. "I guess I'll just call her my little Dee-Dee."

He really thinks Destino is his baby, I thought. Suddenly, a strange feeling crept over me as I watched David. I realized then that he was very naive and I wondered what disappointments, if any, lay ahead for all three of them. Looking at the tiny baby, I considered whether Verónica had willingly stepped inside an invisible, but nonetheless binding, wall of self delusion.

XII

That night I dreamed I was inside a green glass prison, holding Destino on my lap. Strangers were peering at us, waving bits of paper in their hands, their mouths forming sounds I could not hear. I looked at one face after another impassively, wondering who those people were, amazed that they felt compelled to convey a message, a wish perhaps, to Destino and me. Suddenly a space opened up among the crowd and Verónica was making her way through the path.

As she crashed through the glass to get to us, the voice of the crowd rang out in a booming sound, "*¡Esmeralda! ¡Esmeralda!*"

"I'm taking my Destino with me. From now on, she will always be by my side," Verónica whispered as she picked up the baby, then made her way outside again. The crowds pushed against her but one way or another she made her way through them. Once she was out in the open, someone shouted, "She's gone!" And the masses ran after Verónica, trying in vain to catch up with her. "*¡Esmeralda!*" they called. "Don't leave us, *Esmeralda*. What will we do without you?"

Alone at last, inside the glass house, I was fascinated with the walls which slowly began to disintegrate in kaleidoscopic fashion. In place of the green glass, images of flowers and gems flashed past me. Before my eyes, sprigs of dazzling dahlias glided through rubied milk, and saffron-colored sunflowers twirled by on minted teas. I saw clusters of crape myrtle floating on melted jade; and slowly all traces of the glass prison disappeared. I found myself, instead, inside a house made of golden raffia and in the darkness, a topaz presence began to glow. Sunbursts of volcanic warmth emanated from its center and all around me, copal and creosote burned in clay urns. Humming softly as nocturnal blossoms of the tall *saguaro* filled the room, I gave myself up to the energy of a powerful essence which began to breathe on me. Suddenly, a winsome face emerged out of the darkness and a cinnamon-colored stranger smiled at me as he offered me half an orange and a handful of freshly-cut cactus fruits. I smiled back, reaching out for his gifts.

Zulema

Solamente una vez
Amé en la vida
. . .
Una vez, nada más,
se entrega el alma
con la dulce y total
renunciación.

Popular Mexican Song

every three minutes
every five minutes
every ten minutes
every day
women's bodies are found
in alleys & bedrooms
at the top of the stairs

Ntozake Shange

The Cárdenas-Mendoza Family

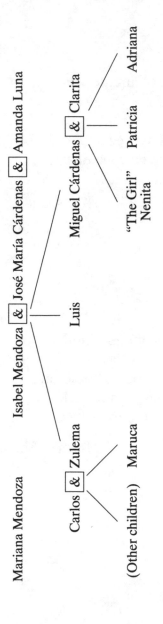

Zulema

I

The story Zulema heard that November morning in 1914 changed her forever, and for the rest of her life she had to deal with the consequences of what she was told on that long-ago Tuesday morning. All during the previous night she had listened to sporadic gunshots across the river where the *Federales* were shooting at the *Villistas*. The noise and the unfamiliar bed had made her wake up long before the bells of San Agustín Church pealed their daily calling to the faithful, and at six o'clock when the first sounds from the belfry echoed in the distance, Zulema got up, blessed herself, then knelt down to say her morning prayers. She heard her aunt Mariana moving around in the next room and wondered if the disturbances in the night had also made her get up earlier than usual.

Mariana looked different that morning, puffy around the eyes and rather tense as she prepared the coffee and tortillas. Zulema sensed she had interrupted her aunt as she came into the kitchen but Mariana instinctively left her *comal* to kiss the child. "I have a lot to tell you," Mariana whispered as she put her arms around Zulema's slender body. Then, as she moved back to the stove and stirred the chocolate she was preparing for the child, Mariana told her the story.

Her voice sounded a little forced and her face looked weary. Zulema would later try to recall the scene but all

she could remember was Mariana's palor and the voice that
had been pitched higher than normal. In this tone Mariana
had told her that her new brother had arrived during the
night, tired from his journey but happy and fat and kicking
with gusto.

The night had been full of activity, she continued, for
not only had the new baby arrived and the shooting continued on the other side but a messenger had also come from
San Antonio. He had informed Zulema's mother that her
other sister, Carmen, had come down with a serious case of
pneumonia. Isabel had left right away with the messenger,
leaving her new-born baby behind with the rest of the family. "Give my Zulemita and Miguelito a kiss and tell them
I'll be home soon." Those had been her last words as she
departed, Mariana said.

"You will stay with me for a while," she continued. Miguel would stay with his father and his grandmother, and
the baby would remain with Dona Julia who lived across the
street and also had a small infant she was nursing. It had all
been arranged.

II

Thirty-five years later, sitting on some thick pillows Zulema had special-made for me, I heard many different versions of what I later realized was the same story. During
my afternoon visits I listened to Zulema'a calm, deep voice
as she invented one tale after another with superbly eccen-
tric characters who continued to dance and whirl about in
my own accelerated imagination. Some of the stories were
simple duplications of tales Mariana had told her but most
of the narratives were Zulema's own inventions. Often Mariana would join us, sitting on the rocking chair with her

eyes closed as though she were reliving the episodes which Zulema was describing.

Now and then Mariana would open her eyes, then lean forward to listen more closely. Then, she would shake her head and correct Zulema. *"No, no fue así,"* and she would turn to me with her own version of the story I had just heard. It was difficult for me to decide whose narrative I liked the most, for they each had their way with description and knew just when to pause for the maximum of effect but I suppose at that time I tended to think that Mariana's *"bola de años,"* as she referred to her advancing age, gave her an edge over Zulema's rendition.

I soon learned that Zulema had a favorite story. It was the one about the camp follower Victoriana, who, at the height of the revolution, had crossed to this side to wait for her lover Joaquín. For a while people coming from her pueblo in Zacatecas confirmed her belief that Joaquín was still alive but as the years passed, everyone simply forgot about Victoriana. She continued her vigil until that unexpected afternoon when the people had found her thirty years later, sitting in the same chair where she had first sat down to wait, covered with cobwebs and red dust but with a glowing expression on her face and her rusted rifle at her feet.

I never got tired of Zulema's *cuento*, for each time she'd recite it, she would pretend it was the first time she had confided to me about Victoriana and she would embellish the story with a few more details. The climax was always the same, though, as she'd describe how Victoriana was unable to recognize the man whose memory she had loved all those years, for when the newspapers had printed the story about her long wait, out of curiosity, Joaquín had come to see Victoriana and she had not singled him out from all the other visitors she had greeted that afternoon. No longer the *campesino* she had fallen in love with but a very important businessman, Joaquín was alternately amused and mortified by all of the moths and butterflies entangled among the cobwebs in her silvered hair.

Zulema would conclude the story with Victoriana boarding the Ferrocarriles Nacionales Mexicanos, while the townspeople waved a sad farewell to the splendid and flamboyant figure who had enlivened their routine lives for a brief while. She, too, waved to the people as the train pulled away, taking her back to her *pueblo* where she hoped to locate some of the relatives she had last seen in Bachimba, claiming their rifles and riding off into the distance to be swept into the force of the revolution.

Unknown endings, unfinished lives. That was the subject of most of Zulema's narratives but I cannot remember when I first began to notice this. On the day after my sixth birthday I sensed something different, for Zulema changed the story from fantasy to biography and for the first time mentioned Isabel to me. She took a photograph from her missal and passed the edge-worn picture to me. "Do you know who she is?"

Immediately I recognized the photo as a copy of one my mother had. "*Es tu mamá*," I responded right away. "*Mi abuelita Isabel*."

I often opened the top drawer of my mother's dresser just to steal a peep at the young woman in the tucked lace blouse who looked back at me with soft, gentle eyes. No one had ever told me much about her except that she was my father's mother who had died when my uncle Luis was born. Each of the boys had been reared by different relatives who did not find it appropriate to talk to them about Isabel, possibly to spare the children from the memories the adults did not want them to have. Up to then I knew very little about her.

"She died when she was only twenty-four. I was six then," Zulema spoke very deliberately. " Mariana really pulled the wool over my eyes, telling me Mamá had gone away with Tía Carmen."

Zulema's shoulders began to rise up and down. Suddenly she started to sob uncontrollably, holding the photo to her breast. Through my own tears I heard her describe how she had waited for days on end for her mother's return during that first winter when Isabel had gone away without a word to her. The minute she'd hear people pass by on the street she'd run to the door on the chance her mother would be with them. The streetcar that clanged in front of the house seemed to sound especially for her and every time she'd see Julia nursing the baby she'd wonder if Luisito was hungry for his own mother. Feeling abandoned she began to talk about her feelings; yet, everyone maintained the story which Mariana had uttered. When, when, when she had asked her aunt, and Mariana had finally said, "When the war is over, she'll be back."

And so the eight-year old Zulema had become interested in the war. At night whenever she heard gunshots or sirens she'd cry herself to sleep. The bugles of the infantry across the river woke her up every morning and in the afternoons after class she'd go down to the river to look across its banks at the war-weary nation on the other side. Then she would wish the war away, praying with her eyes closed while she imagined her mother running towards her with outstretched arms. But Zulema could sense that Isabel would not be back for a long time, for every day she was aware of the dozens of people who crossed the bridge with their belongings in wheelbarrows or in suitcases of every sort. Some even had knapsacks slung across their back, looking tired and worn from the personal anxieties they too were experiencing. Sometimes her father would give work around the store or at the ranch to some of the people who had just arrived, and before they moved on farther north, Zulema would take advantage of their personal accounts to ask them questions about the war. No one had any idea when the fighting would end and many of them no longer cared about the revolution except for the manner in which it had altered the course of their lives. They were mostly preoccupied with the death and destruction over which they had absolutely no control.

With all the talk of death, Zulema soon became apprehensive. When the newly-arrived talked about the death of their loved ones, she began to associate their experiences with her own loss and slowly began to doubt the story about her mother's return. On her ninth birthday, in 1917, she had let everyone know she realized the war was supposed to be over and still her mother had not come back. "I know she is lost," she concluded. Then she looked directly at Mariana and stated in a tone of finality. "I no longer have a mother."

And that same day she had started to tell her own stories. She took Miguelito and Luisito to her room and sat them down on the floor, while she lay on her bed looking up at the ceiling. *"Les voy a contar un cuento de nunca acabar,"* she began, then started to narrate her own version of the Sleeping Beauty, who had been put under a spell by her wicked stepmother. Sleeping Beauty was supposed to be awakened by the kiss of a gorgeous prince but that never really happened. She turned to her brothers and asked them if they knew why the prince had not found Sleeping Beauty. Then, without giving them a chance to answer, for this was supposed to be her very own story, she continued with melodramatic gestures.

The prince could not find Sleeping Beauty, she whispered, because a revolution broke out just as he was setting out on his journey. Word soon arrived that his white horse had been confiscated by Emiliano Zapata. So now the prince had to find his way around on foot, and not being accustomed to looking out for himself, he had no idea what direction he should take. Finally, he headed towards his castle but when he got there he found that it had been blown to pieces, and the revolutionaries had proclaimed that he could no longer be a prince. And so he was unable to complete his mission. Poor Sleeping Beauty was left forgotten in the woods but since she could not live without the prince, for they needed each other to exist, she simply had no future and remained out there in the dark woods forever and ever. Pretty soon no one could remember, much less care, about the troubles of that poor little Sleeping Beauty, foolish enough to think she needed to live with a prince in a castle. So, without realizing what they had done, the revolutionaries got rid of all those charming princes and the silly, pampered Sleeping Beauties as well.

That afternoon I listened for a long time as Zulema recited one such story after another. From the beginning, she said, her brothers did not like her plots because they considered her endings to be strange, even morbid at times. Once in a while she had tried to tell her stories to her father but he did not seem the least bit interested in them. Mariana, who perhaps best understood what she was really trying to say, assumed she could change her endings. So, for lack of an audience Zulema felt she had been fated to keep them to herself all those years. I was the only one who had let her tell the stories the way she wanted.

"Zulema, I like your stories," I reassured her as I undid her braids, then ran my small fingers through her hair.

I then looked at her in a whole new way. Unlike Mariana and the picture we had of Isabel, Zulema seemed quite ordinary, with her long hair parted in the middle and plaited into thick braids which she wore criss-crossed on top of her head. She did not look like my mother either, whose hair was swept up, away from her face and wrapped around a hair piece that was pinned around her head in keeping with the fashion of the day. I much preferred Zulema's hair, which I loved to unbraid, then brush out in waves which reached down to her waist.

That afternoon I gave her particular attention weaving a red satin ribbon into her braids which made her look prettier than usual. Finally animated, she continued with the narrative that had gone unshared all those years. She skipped the elaboration she gave to her other tales and was direct and terse as she described the main event that had shaped her life. She really could not blame Mariana or her father, she said, for they had simply been trying to save her from the very pain they had inadvertently caused. By the time she was twelve she had given up altogether on her mother's return although occasionally when she opened a door in her father's house, for an instant she felt she had caught a glimpse of her mother sitting there in her rocking chair. That was about the time she took to leaving all the doors in the house ajar. Gradually she became fascinated with opening trunks and boxes as well.

One day while she was visiting her father and Amanda, she found herself alone in the room where he kept his papers. Slowly, she began to poke into his desk and in a drawer, underneath some photos, she uncovered the announcement which she unknowingly had been searching for all those months. She picked up the card, looked at its black borders, then read: *ISABEL MENDOZA-DEL VALLE, esposa de José María Cárdenas—1890–1914.* The rest of the announcement stated that Isabel was survived by three children—Zulema, Miguel and Luis.

Zulema put the card back where she had found it. After that she lost her interest in rummaging through boxes and drawers. She began to rise at six o'clock in order to attend daily mass where she remained until it was time for school. Gradually she began to lose interest in her classes, and one day she decided to stay in church all day. For several weeks she sat in the immense church where the incense soothed her memories and the candles she lit brightened the semi-darkness. Soon *el Padre Salinas* began to notice the disappearance of the candles. Concerned that almost no money was being left in the offering box to cover their cost, he staked out the various altars and, shortly thereafter, caught her sitting in the front pew facing the virgin and child. He watched as she lighted two or three candles at once, then when those burned down, he saw her light new ones.

Just about the time *el Padre Salinas* approached Mariana about the expense, the teacher paid José María a visit. José María did not take the trouble to discuss the matter with his daughter; instead, he talked to Mariana who related to Zulema that her father now wished to keep her at home, for she could no longer be trusted to go out on her own. From then on she would not be allowed to go anywhere without being accompanied either by one of the cousins or the aunts.

Zulema had not minded the restrictions at all. In fact, for the first time she felt she was the object of everyone's attention. Mariana taught her the secrets that went into cooking traditional dishes. For their *mole de gallina* they would spend a good part of a day grinding sesame seeds, peanuts and *pastillas de chocolate* on the *metate* and once the ingredients for the sauce were ready, they would simmer it for hours. It was then that they would go to the chicken coop to pick out two or three chickens. At first Zulema was squeamish but she soon learned to wring a chicken by the neck before chopping off its head with a *machete*. For dessert she loved to make *capirotada* and *leche quemada* and the first time she prepared the entire meal for a table of twelve, she relished all the compliments she got for her *calabaza con puerco*.

Doña Julia taught her to crochet, little squares at first, then larger items like tablecloths and bedspreads which she made as gifts for *fiestas de quinceañeras*, engagement showers and weddings. When she turned fifteen she too was honored with a dance attended by all the relatives, their friends and friends of her father. Everyone danced to the music of a local band until the early hours of the morning and between dances they kept going back for more *tamales* and steaming cups of cinnamoned coffee. Before the night was over, all the spread on the table —*barbacoa, guacamole, arroz, frijoles borrachos* and freshly grilled *gorditas*—had been eaten up.

That was the first time she had met Carlos who danced all evening with her. A few days later, he had called on her father requesting permission to visit with her at home. Soon she began to be kidded about having a sweetheart and when the *comadres* in Maríana's quilt-making group asked her about Carlos, Zulema smiled and pretended to be concentrating on her stitches. After a while, she filled her trunk with the essentials for her future life and when she married Carlos, she brought to her new home all the exquisite handmade items that a seventeen-year old bride needed. A few weeks after Zulema's and Carlos's first child was born, Mariana came to live with them, and for more than twenty years the three of them saw the family expand, then contract again, as the older sons went off to study at the university and the youngest daughter married, at seventeen, like her mother.

Zulema had tried to get each one of her children interested in listening to her stories but all four thought the stories were silly and repetitive. So, it wasn't until I started making requests for recitations about her extravagant characters that she began to ponder about this particular vacuum in her life.

Now, as the afternoon light softly faded, Zulema paused to reflect on everything she had told me. Finally, she sighed, "Telling stories. That's what I've enjoyed the most."

"Me too," I smiled, tucking at her red ribbons.

Just then the door opened and my cousin Maruca turned on the light. Surprised, she asked "How come you're sitting in the dark?"

Neither of us answered her. Then, she burst out, "*Ay, Mamá*, why are you wearing those silly ribbons? You look as if you were about to dance *el jarabe tapatío.*"

"She looks great with her hair like this," I responded.

Maruca waved her hand as if to brush my comment aside. "You two live in your special little world, with all your *cuentos*. Come join us now. I've brought a big trayful of fried chicken and potato salad."

"We'll come in a minute," Zulema answered. "Just let us finish here."

As soon as we were alone again, Zulema looked at me very intently, tapping her index finger against her mouth. "Nenita, let's keep this to ourselves. Poor Mariana. It's been such a long time since mother died. There's no point in creating problems now. All this was just between you and me, okay?"

III

Earlier that day, my sister Patricia had called to inform me about the heart attack. In my rush to the bus station I had forgotten my sunglasses and the bright light of the afternoon was now blinding me. Closing my eyes, I tried to sort out my feelings but I couldn't focus on anything. Instead, I tried leafing through the magazine I had picked up at the Greyhound shop. News of Czechoslovakia, Viet Nam and Cambodia flashed by me. A picture of Joan Baez. Many anti-war demonstrators. Unable to concentrate, I set the magazine aside.

Leaning against the bus window I stretched out my legs across the two seats and studied the passengers closest to me. Two rows up on my left was a woman with very teased hair. She reminded me of Florinda's Cuban mother whom I knew only through my sister's vivid description. I looked around at the other people, then fidgeted with the journal I had on my lap. Feeling its smooth leather cover, I remembered how pleased I had been the previous Christmas when Mariana and Zulema had given it to me. On its first page, they had inscribed: "Make this a memory book of your very own dreams and aspirations." It was the first thing I grabbed when I started to pack for this journey home but at the moment I did not feel like looking at it.

I concentrated instead on the woman with the teased hair. Florinda's mother must have looked like that when she left Cuba ten years ago. In anticipation of the day when the family would leave the island, she had let her hair grow for more than a year. Then when the moment for their departure arrived, she had carefully teased her hair, then divided it into three layers. The first section had been twisted into a tight French roll fastened with pins encrusted with precious gems. A small fortune I was told. The tiny twist had been covered with a larger one held up by more jeweled hairpins. Finally, the top outer layer neatly covering the cache, had been sprayed several times with a heavy lacquer. As if to mock fate, she had attached thin wires with pink and white gauze butterflies all over her hair. According to my sister, Florinda had said that her mother looked so outrageous no one bothered much with her and she had smuggled a sizeable sum which the family had used to set up a fabric store. Several years later, it was a thriving business.

For reasons I didn't quite understand, Florinda's mother's story always made me anxious. So, I lit a cigarette and watched the smoke whirl upwards. From the angle the sun was hitting me, the smoke resembled the tumultuous vapors in the film version of 'Pedro Páramo.' In that film, as Juan Preciado searched for his father, the vapors kept getting thicker and thicker the more he travelled inside the land of the dead.

"This is my favorite novel," I had pointed out to Zulema and Mariana on the previous Thanksgiving holiday. "But I'm sure there's a lot in this novel I don't understand," I had warned as I introduced them to the spirits, the *espíritus*, of Comala.

We had been reading from the paperback copies of *Pedro Páramo* that I had given to each of them. Mariana and I did most of the reading, although Zulema sometimes took her turn. Sipping Cuervo *añejo*, we had commented on the novel, pointing out the scenes we had particularly enjoyed. Mariana, especially, was enthralled with the characters at the Rancho Media Luna, for they were part of a period she still remembered well. And Zulema, as I had expected, identified with Susana, the character whose fate had also been shaped by the early death of her mother.

"The spirits always continue to influence those who live after them," Mariana had sighed. "Just right here, we have the example of Zulema, who suffered so much after the death of Isabel."

Zulema and I had glanced at one another. Fifty-five years after the death of her sister, Mariana was finally commenting on it.

"Why do you say that?" I had softly questioned.

"It's just that the murmurs get stronger by the day," she had answered, extending her hands on the armrest. She had closed her eyes rocking herself back and forth letting us know the conversation had ended for the moment. Finally, she had murmured, "It is time now" and to our astonishment she said she would take us to Isabel's burial place.

As I drove to the cemetery in silence, my mind was full of questions. Like the rest of the family, I had succumbed to the story of Isabel's departure and had not even asked where she had been buried. For twenty years, since Zulema had told me her version of her mother's death, I had learned to think of Isabel as a spirit living the special life of the dead. I wondered if Zulema was as shocked as I was since she too had not uttered a word.

"Vamos por este camino." Mariana led us through the old part of the cemetery to an enclosed plot. There, a red tin can with a cluster of marigolds lay half-buried in front of a tombstone marked with the same inscription as on the death announcement which Zulema had read so long ago: *ISABEL MENDOZA-DEL VALLE, 1890-1914.*

I was stunned, realizing that for all these years, Isabel had been within reach. Zulema's lower lip started to tremble and little whimpering sounds began to come out of her mouth. Mariana put her arm around Zulema's shoulder, then rested her head on it.

"I never knew how to remedy what had happened," Mariana said simply. It was obvious she finally wanted to break the silence surrounding Isabel and in order to get her off her feet, we moved to a nearby bench.

For a while we sat quietly. Then Mariana began to tell us about the difficulty she had experienced in repeating the story the family had chosen for the children on the night Isabel had died. From the very beginning she had made adjustments in her life, for she had stayed home with Zulema while the rest of the family attended the novena for her sister. Later, when the child's suspicions were aroused, she had started to doubt the decision to protect Zulema from the truth.

Yet, after a few years they themselves had almost accepted the story as fact and tacitly believed it would be much more difficult to adjust to a new reality than to live with the pattern that had been set. "I didn't know what to do," Mariana repeated over and over.

Then she told us about her weekly visits to the cemetery and how she considered those visits her personal ritual in keeping the memory of Isabel alive. For years she had snuck away on the bus with her little bouquet of marigolds. But, as she got older, her visits became more and more sporadic. Still, only a few days before, she had brought the flowers we had just seen.

I looked at Mariana's rheumatic limbs and wondered how she had managed to honor her sister for so long.

"Uno hace lo que tiene que hacer," she affirmed as they headed back to the car. I repeated those words to myself, "One simply does what one has to do."

For the rest of the day I tried to fit together all the pieces of the story and started to write long entries about Mariana, Isabel and Zulema in a loose-leaf journal. When I got back to my apartment I continued writing and one day in early December, I stuffed my notes into an envelope and mailed it off to them, with instructions to save the pages for me. A few weeks after that, they gave me my blue leatherbound book as a present.

I reached over to feel it, then opened my eyes. We had arrived. As soon as we pulled into the terminal I saw my sister Patricia waiting for me.

"How is she doing?" I asked.

"She's been hanging on but she won't last much longer. Late this morning she had another heart attack and the doctor does not think she'll pull through this time."

IV

As I opened the door I heard Father Murphy reciting the prayers of Extreme Unction and saw him blessing the small body on the hospital bed. My mother leaned towards me and whispered as she put her arm around me, "I'm so sorry. She died about fifteen minutes ago."

I felt everyone's eyes on me as I walked up to the bed. As tears streamed down my face I kissed the smooth sallow cheeks, then looked at the body for a long time without saying anything. It was useless for me to remain there, I thought, and slowly I began to envision what it was I had to do.

In my sister's car I drove across the border to the church by the first plaza, then walked towards the adjacent small shop which sold religious articles. As I had hoped, its window display was full of saints with tin *milagros* pinned to their clothing. Inside I found hundreds of *milagros* for sale in many different shapes, sizes and materials. Immediately I by-passed the larger ones and the gold ones which I could not afford. Looking at the half-inch tin offerings, I carefully selected from those in the shape of human profiles, hearts and tongues of fire. The volunteer at the shop seemed surprised when I said I wanted five dozen of each, then waited patiently while I made my selection. Eventually, she divided the offerings into small plastic bags.

With the *milagros* on my lap I drove a few blocks to the flower market. There I purchased bunches of marigolds and asked the vendor to divide them up into small bouquets which he tied together with white ribbons. They took up most of the back seat, making the custom inspector remark on my collection of *flores para los muertos*. My next stop was the stationery shop where I bought a small box of red cinnamon-scented candles. Then, on my way to the funeral parlor I passed by a record shop. Slamming on the brakes, I double-parked and ran in to inquire if they sold small 45's that were blank. The clerk thought they had three such records left over from an old special order. As soon as he found them I rushed back to the car and made my way to the funeral parlor. The administrator listened rather dubiously to my plans, then reluctantly gave me permission to do as I wished.

I went home to rest for a while, then at the agreed-upon hour I returned to the funeral parlor and for the next three hours I carried out my task. My back hurt from being bent for so long as, between tears, I carefully sewed the *milagros* on the white satin which lined the inside cover of the casket. Applying three stitches through the tiny hole on each tin sculpture I made a design of three arcs—the faces were on the outer row, the tongues in the middle and the hearts on the inner row. Once I finished with the *milagros* I stepped back to get a better view. Seeing how pretty they looked, each with its accompanying tiny red ribbon, I cried once more, yet felt a little relief from my sorrow knowing that when the lid was closed *the milagros* would be a lovely sight to behold from inside. Then, with the marigolds, I created a halo effect on the space above the corpse, hoping its spirit could savor the smell of the flowers. I arranged the candles in a row in front of the casket and felt myself tremble as I placed the three records on the left side of the body. "*Llénalos con tus cuentos favoritos,*" I whispered. "Fill them with your favorite stories."

For a long time I sat in the semi-darkness, mesmerized by the smell of the flowers and the perfumed glow of the candles. Recalling the many *cuentos* which had inspired my youthful imagination, I felt I could stay there forever. But I knew I did not want to see anyone tonight, and soon someone would be coming to sit out the early morning vigil.

Slowly, I got up and walked to the coffin once again. The *milagros* and the flowers looked splendid but I wondered what the rest of the family would say when they saw them. I touched the dear figure for the last time, then walked out into the night knowing I would not be going to the burial ceremony the next afternoon.

Instead I went home and immediately began to write in my journal. For two days I wrote, filling all its pages. Then I gave my thick blue book to Patricia so she could read what

I had just finished.

She started reading right away and did not move from her chair for hours. At times I would see her shake her head and make almost audible sounds. Finally, when she finished, she closed the book but kept her hand on its cover.

"*No*," she said. "*No fue así*." A stern expression crossed her face. "It's not been at all the way you've presented it. You've mixed up some of the stories Mariana and Zulema have told you, which might not even be true in the first place. I've heard other versions from Tía Carmen and, in fact, from Zulema herself. Mariana would never even recognize herself if you ever show this to her."

"I'm not sure what you are trying to do," Patricia continued, but what you have here is not at all what really happened."

"*Lo que tienes aquí no es lo que pasó*."

I smiled at Patricia, then took my journal back. As I did so, I remembered that my mother always said that her own memory book had been a collection of images of our family's past both as it was and as we all would have liked that past to have been.

"You know," I responded. "*Uno cuenta de la feria según lo que ve en ella*. Each of us tell it as we see it."

GLOSSARY

(Translations prepared by the author)

Andrea

jota aragonesa	a type of Spanish dance
No te metas más en ese mundo.	Don't get further involved in that world.
¡Bienvenidas!	Welcome!
Qué gusto verlos.	What a pleasure to see them.
Por desgracia.	Through bad luck.

Amanda

¿Dónde está el niño que yo fui/ sigue dentro de mí o se fue?	What has happened to the child that I was/ Is she still inside of me or is she gone?
. . .	. . .
¿Por qué anduvimos tanto tiempo creciendo para separarnos?	Why did we spend so much time together only to go on our separate ways?
lentejuelas de conchanacar	sequins made out of mother-of-pearl
¿Te gusta, muchacha?	Do you like it, girl?

Filomena

zempoalxochitles (a nahuatl, not a Spanish term)	chrysanthemum-type flowers
¡Flores para los muertos!	Flowers for the dead!
El 2 de noviembre—Día de los Muertos	November 2—the Day of the Dead
¡Loro! ¡Loro! ¡Loro!	Parrot! Parrot! Parrot!
Mira, nomás.	Oh, my! Just look.
Requiescat in pacem.	Rest in peace.
Así lo quiere Dios.	That's the will of God.
Trois contes	Three Tales

Leonor

luminarias	paper bags illuminated with candles set on sand
fandangos	festive entertainment
Un peligroso	A dangerous one
ocotillo	a type of pine tree from Mexico
Es la cruz de Quetzalcóatl.	It's Quetzalcoatl's cross.
Lo mismo de siempre.	The same as always.
políticos	politicians

Esmeralda

"Solamente una vez/ Amé en la vida	"Only once/ Have I loved
. . .	. . .
Una vez, nada más,/ se entrega el alma/ con la dulce y total/ renunciación."	Only once, only then,/ Can one love completely/ With a yielding submission/ That is both sweet and total."
Una esmeralda brillante	a brillant emerald
"Verde, que te quiero verde."	"Green, I want you green." (from a poem by the Spanish poet Federico García Lorca)
Piropos.	Compliments.
Dulce. Muy dulce.	Sweet. Very sweet.
ocotillo	a type of pine tree from Mexico
saguaro	a type of cactus plant
En mi casa no tolero puterías.	In my home, I will not tolerate the ways of whores.
huila-daughter	fucking daughter
Híjole	Shit
yerba del oso	cow parsnip
maravilla	four-o'clock
romerillo	silver sage
pegapega	evening star

Ándale.	Go on.
Anímala.	Cheer her up.
Lloronas, todas.	Wailing women, all of us.
picardía	[In this instance]: open sexual expression
comadre	woman-buddy
¡Caray!	Oh, my!
norteña	northern (referring to northern Mexico)
merienda	a tea-type afternoon party

Zulema

No, no fue así.	No, it wasn't like that.
bola de años	accumulating years
cuento	story
campesino	peasant
pueblo	small town
Es tu mamá. Mi abuelita Isabel.	It's your mother. My grandmother Isabel.
Les voy a contar un cuento de nunca acabar	Once upon a time …
esposa de José María Cárdenas	wife of José María Cárdenas

mole de gallina	chicken *mole* (a Pre-Columbian dish)
pastillas de chocolate	large chocolate tablets
metate	a grinding stone
capirotada & leche quemada	types of dessert: bread pudding & caramelized milk
calabaza con puerco	pork and squash dish
fiestas de quinceañeras	birthday parties for fifteen-year-old girls
barbacoa, guacamole, arroz, frijoles borrachos ... gorditas	barbacued meat, *guacamole*, rice, beans cooked in beer ... extra thick *tortillas*
comadres	women buddies
el jarabe tapatío	Mexican hat dance
cuentos	stories
Vamos por este camino.	Let's go this way.
milagros	small sculptural religious offerings
flores para los muertos	flowers for the dead
No fue así.	It wasn't this way.